Humor, Quotes and Inspiration

Wit and Wisdom for Writers and Speakers

Compiled by Bobby Huguley

ISBN: 9798623859556

In memory of Bill Zerfass (1929-2019), Friend, Colleague, Mentor, and lover of funny stories.

Cover art by Graham Culbertson

CONTENTS

For my wife Marsha

For Paul, Stephanie, Solomon, and Lydia Huguley

For Andrea, Graham, Reid, and Micah Culbertson

And for all the church choir members with whom I've been privileged to serve

Animals

Advantages of Having a Dog

- It doesn't take 45 minutes to get a dog ready to go outside in the winter.
- Dogs cannot lie.
- Dogs never resist nap time.
- You don't need to get extra phone lines for a dog.
- Dogs don't pester you about getting a kid.
- Dogs don't care if the peas have been touched by the mashed potatoes.
- Average cost of sending a dog to school: $42…
- Average cost of sending a kid: $153,000….
- Dogs are housebroken by the time they are 12 weeks old.
- Your dog is not embarrassed if you sing in public.
- If your dog is a bad seed, your genes cannot be blamed.

Concise Telegraph

A German shepherd went to a Western Union office, took out a blank form and wrote, "Woof. Woof. Woof. Woof. Woof. Woof. Woof. Woof. Woof."

The clerk examined the paper and told the dog, "There are only nine words here. You could send another "woof" for the same price."

"But," the dog replied, "that would be silly."

Explanation of Life

On the first day, God created the dog and said: "Sit all day by the door of your house and bark at anyone who comes in or walks past. For this, I will give you a life span of twenty years."

The dog said: "That's a long time to be barking. How about only ten years and I'll give you back the other ten?"

So God agreed.

On the second day, God created the monkey and said: "Entertain people, do tricks, and make them laugh. For this, I'll give you a twenty-year life span."

The monkey said: "Monkey tricks for twenty years? That's a pretty long time to perform. How about I give you back ten like the Dog did?"

And God agreed.

On the third day, God created the cow and said: "You must go into the field with the farmer all day long and suffer under the sun, have calves and give milk to support the farmer's family. For this, I will give you a life span of sixty years."

The cow said: "That's kind of a tough life you want me to live for sixty years. How about twenty and I'll give back the other forty?"

And God agreed again.

On the fourth day, God created man and said: "Eat, sleep, play, marry and enjoy your life. For this, I'll give you twenty years."

But man said: "Only twenty years? Could you possibly give me my twenty, the forty the cow gave back, the ten the monkey gave back, and the ten the dog gave back; that makes eighty, okay?"

"Okay," said God, "You asked for it."

So that is why for our first twenty years we eat, sleep, play and enjoy ourselves. For the next forty years we slave in the sun to support our family. For the next ten years we do monkey tricks to entertain the grandchildren. And for the last ten years we sit on the front porch and bark at everyone.

Faithful Ostrich

A man walks into a restaurant with a full-grown ostrich behind him, and as he sits down, the waitress comes over and asks for their order.

The man says, "I'll have a hamburger, fries and a coke," and turns to the ostrich. "What's yours?"

"I'll have the same," says the ostrich.

A short time later the waitress returns with the order. "That will be $6.40 please," and the man reaches into his pocket and pulls out exact change for payment.

The next day, the man and the ostrich come again and the man says, "I'll have a hamburger, fries and a coke," and the ostrich says, "I'll have the same." Once again, the man reaches into his pocket and pays with exact change.

This becomes a routine until late one evening, the two enter again.

"The usual?" asks the waitress.

"No, this is Friday night, so I will have a steak, baked potato and salad," says the man. "Same for me," says the ostrich.

A short time later the waitress comes with the order and says, "That will be $12.62."

Once again, the man pulls exact change out of his pocket and places it on the table. The waitress can't hold back her curiosity any longer.

"Excuse me, sir. How do you manage to always come up with the exact change out of your pocket every time?"

"Well," says the man, "several years ago I was cleaning the attic and I found an old lamp. When I rubbed it, a Genie appeared and offered me two wishes. My first wish was that if I ever had to pay for anything, just put my hand in my pocket, and the right amount of money would always be there."

"That's brilliant!" says the waitress. "Most people would wish for a million dollars or something, but you'll always be as rich as you want for as long as you live!"

"That's right! Whether it's a gallon of milk or a Rolls Royce, the exact money is always there," says the man.

The waitress asks, "One other thing, sir, what's with the ostrich?"

The man sighs, pauses, and answers, "My second wish was for a tall chick with long legs who agrees with everything I say."

Help Wanted

A local business was looking for office help. They put a sign in the window, stating the following: "HELP WANTED. Must be able to type, must be good with a computer and must be bilingual. We are an Equal Opportunity Employer."

A short time afterwards, a dog trotted up to the window, saw the sign and went inside. He looked at the receptionist and wagged his tail, then walked over to the sign, looked at it and whined. Getting the idea, the receptionist got the office manager. The office manager looked at the dog and was surprised, to say the least. However, the dog looked determined, so he led him into the office. Inside, the dog jumped up on the chair and stared at the manager.

The manager said, "I can't hire you. The sign says you have to be able to type."

The dog jumped down, went to the typewriter and proceeded to type out a perfect letter. He took out the page and trotted over to the manager and gave it to him, then jumped back on the chair.

The manager was stunned, but then told the dog, "The sign says you have to be good with a computer."

The dog jumped down again and went to the computer. The dog proceeded to enter and execute a perfect program, that worked flawlessly the first time. By this time the manager was totally dumbfounded!

He looked at the dog and said, "I realize that you are a very intelligent dog and have some interesting abilities. However, I still can't give you the job." The dog jumped down and went to a copy of the sign and put his paw on the sentences that told about being an Equal Opportunity Employer.

The manager said, "Yes, but the sign also says that you have to be bilingual".

The dog looked at the manager calmly and said, "Meow".

How are you feeling?

Farmer Roscoe decided his injuries from the accident were serious enough to take the trucking company (responsible for the accident) to court. In court the trucking company's fancy lawyer was questioning farmer Roscoe.

"Didn't you say, at the scene of the accident, 'I'm fine'?" said the lawyer.

Farmer Roscoe responded, "Well I'll tell you what happened. I had just loaded my favorite mule Bessie into the...."

"I didn't ask for any details," the lawyer interrupted, "just answer the question." "Did you not say, at the scene of the accident, 'I'm fine!"

Farmer Roscoe said, "Well I had just got Bessie into the trailer and I was driving down the road...."

The lawyer interrupted again and said, "Judge, I am trying to establish the fact that, at the scene of the accident, this man told the Highway Patrolman that he was just fine. Now several weeks after the accident he is trying to sue my client. I believe he is a fraud. Please tell him to simply answer the question."

By this time the Judge was fairly interested in Farmer Roscoe's answer and said to the lawyer, "I'd like to hear that he has to say about his favorite mule Bessie."

Roscoe thanked the Judge and proceeded, "Well as I was saying, I had just loaded Bessie, my favorite mule, into the trailer and was driving her down the highway when this huge semi-truck and trailer ran the stop sign and smacked my truck right in the side. I was thrown into one ditch and Bessie was thrown into the other. I was hurting real bad and didn't want to move. However, I could hear ole Bessie moaning and groaning. I knew she was in terrible shape just by her groans. Shortly after the accident a Highway Patrolman came on the scene. He could hear Bessie moaning and groaning so he went over to her. After he looked at her, he took out his gun and shot her between the eyes. Then the Patrolman came across the road with his gun in his hand and looked at me. He said, "Your mule was in such bad shape I had to shoot her. How are you feeling?"

Parrot Training

Mary received a parrot as a gift. The parrot was fully grown with a very bad attitude and worse vocabulary. Every other word was a cruse: those that weren't curses were to say the least, rude. Mary tried to change the bird's attitude by constantly saying polite things and playing soft music- anything she could think of. Nothing worked. She yelled at the bird and the bird got worse. She shook the bird and the bird got madder and more rude.

Finally, in a moment of desperation, Mary put the parrot in the freezer to get a minute of peace. For a few moments she heard the bird swearing, squawking, kicking, and screaming, and then, suddenly there was absolute quiet. Mary was frightened that she might have actually hurt the bird and quickly opened the freezer door.

The parrot calmly stepped out onto Mary's extended arm and said: "I'm very sorry that I offended you with my language and my actions and I ask your forgiveness. I will endeavor to correct my behavior and I am sure it will never happen again."
Mary was astounded at the changes in the bird's attitude and was about to ask what had changed him, when the parrot continued,

"May I ask what the chicken did?"

Smart Dog

A dog walks into a butcher shop with a purse strapped around his neck. He walks up to the meat case and calmly sits there until it's his turn to be waited on.

A man, who was already in the butcher shop, finished his purchase and noticed the dog. The butcher leaned over the counter and asked the dog what it wanted today. The dog put its paw on the glass case in front of the ground beef, and the butcher said, "How many pounds?"

The dog barked twice, so the butcher made a package of two pounds ground beef.

He then said, "Anything else?" The dog pointed to the pork chops, and the butcher said, "How many?" The dog barked four times, and the butcher made up a package of four pork chops.

The dog then walked around behind the counter, so the butcher could get at the purse. The butcher took out the appropriate amount of money and tied two packages of meat around the dog's neck.

The man, who had been watching all of this, decided to follow the dog. It walked for several blocks and then walked up to a house where it began to scratch the door to be let in. As the owner opened the door, the man said to the owner, "That's a really smart dog you have there."

The owner said, "He's not really all that smart. This is the second time this week he's forgotten his key."

Talking Dog

A man was driving around the back woods of Montana, and saw a sign in front of a broken- down shanty-style house: "Talking Dog For Sale." He knocked on the door; and the owner appeared, telling him the dog is in the backyard. The man walked into the backyard, and saw a nice-looking Labrador retriever sitting there.

"You talk?" he asked.

"Yep," the Lab replied.

After the man recovered from the shock of hearing a dog talk, he said "So, what's your story?"

The Lab looked up and said, "Well, I discovered that I could talk when I was pretty young. I wanted to help the government, so I told the CIA. In no time at all they had me jetting from country to country, sitting in rooms with spies and world leaders, because no one figured a dog would be eavesdropping." I was one of their most valuable spies for eight years running. But the jetting around really tired me out, and I knew I wasn't getting any younger, so I decided to settle down. I signed up for a job at the airport to do some undercover security, wandering near suspicious characters and listening in. I uncovered some incredible dealings and was awarded a batch of medals. I got married, had a mess of puppies; and now I'm just retired."

The man was amazed. He returned to the owner, and asked what he wanted for the dog.

"Ten dollars," the owner replied.

"Ten dollars? This dog is amazing! Why on earth are you selling him so cheap?"

"Because he's a liar. He's never been out of the yard."

The Little Turtle

The little turtle climbs the tree very slowly, very painfully. Then she crawls along a branch, to the very end, and when she finally gets to the edge, she jumps. And she falls. But she doesn't get discouraged. So she walks to the tree, she climbs the tree, she crawls along the branch, she gets to the edge, and she jumps, and falls to the ground. Again, with a stubborn look in her face, the little turtle walks slowly to the tree, she climbs the tree, she crawls along the branch, she gets to the edge, and she jumps, and falls.

In a nearby tree a couple of pigeons are looking at the little turtle. Walk, climb, crawl, jump, fall. Over and over again.

After a while one of the pigeons ask the other, "Hey honey, don't you think it's time we tell her that she's adopted?"

Valuable Dog

On a country road, a speeder hit and killed a dog. The dog's owner stood nearby, a gun in his hand.

The speeder said, "Looks as if I killed your dog."

"Sure does."

"I'm sorry. Was it a valuable dog?"

"I wouldn't say that."

"Well, suppose I gave you a hundred dollars. Would that be enough?"

"Well, I don't know."

"Two hundred dollars. That should do it."

"Sounds good."

The speeder reached into his pocket and came up with the money. Pressing it into the man's hand, he said, "I'm sorry I spoiled your plans to go hunting."

"I wasn't going hunting. I was heading out to the woods to shoot that mangy dog."

What is a Cat?
1. Cats do what they want.
2. They rarely listen to you.
3. They're totally unpredictable.
4. When you want to play, they want to be alone.
5. When you want to be alone, they want to play.
6. They expect you to cater to their every whim.
7. They're moody.
8. They leave hair everywhere.

Conclusion: They're tiny women in little fur coats.

What is a Dog?

1. Dogs spend all day sprawled on the most comfortable piece of furniture in the house.
2. They can hear a package of food opening half a block away, but don't hear you when you're in the same room.
3. They can look dumb and lovable all at the same time.
4. They growl when they are not happy.
5. When you want to play, they want to play.
6. When you want to be alone, they want to play.
7. They leave their toys everywhere.
8. They do disgusting things with their mouths and then try to give you a kiss.

Conclusion: They're tiny men in little fur coats.

Wise Old Dog

One day an old German Shepherd starts chasing rabbits and before long, discovers that he's lost. Wandering about, he notices a panther heading rapidly in his direction with the intention of having lunch.

The old German Shepherd thinks, 'Oh, oh! I'm in deep doo-doo now!' Noticing some bones on the ground close by, he immediately settles down to chew on the bones with his back to the approaching cat. Just as the panther is about to leap, the old German Shepherd exclaims loudly, 'Boy, that was one delicious panther! I wonder, if there are any more around here?'

Hearing this, the young panther halts his attack in mid-strike, a look of terror comes over him and he slinks away into the trees. 'Whew!' says the panther, 'That was close! That old German Shepherd nearly had me!'

Meanwhile, a squirrel who had been watching the whole scene

from a nearby tree, figures he can put this knowledge to good use and trade it for protection from the panther. So, off he goes. The squirrel soon catches up with the panther, spills the beans and strikes a deal for himself with the panther. The young panther is furious at being made a fool of and says, 'Here, squirrel, hop on my back and see what's going to happen to that conniving canine!

Now, the old German Shepherd sees the panther coming with the squirrel on his back and thinks, 'What am I am going to do now?', but instead of running, the dog sits down with his back to his attackers, pretending he hasn't seen them yet, and just when they get close enough to hear, the old German Shepherd says...'Where's that squirrel? I sent him off an hour ago to bring me another panther!

<u>Moral of this story</u>...

Don't mess with the old dogs... Age and skill will always overcome youth and treachery!

Bar Humor

Brothers

A cowboy walks into a bar in Texas, orders three mugs of Bud and sits in the back room, drinking a sip out of each one in turn. When he finishes them, he comes back to the bar and orders three more.

The bartender approaches and tells the cowboy, "You know, a mug goes flat after I draw it, it would taste better if you bought one at a time."

The cowboy replies, "Well you see, I have two brothers. One is in Australia, the other is in Dublin, and I'm in Texas. When we all left home, we promised that we'd drink this way to remember the days we drank together. So I drink one for each of my brothers and one for myself."

The bartender admits that this is a nice custom, and leaves it there. The cowboy becomes a regular in the bar, and always drinks the same way. He orders three mugs and drinks them in turn.

One day, he comes in and orders two mugs. All the regulars take notice and fall silent. When he comes back to the bar for the second round, the bartender says, "I don't want to intrude on your grief, but I wanted to offer my condolences on your loss."

The cowboy looks quite puzzled for a moment, then it dawns on him, and he laughs. "Oh, no, everybody's just fine," he explains, "It's just that my wife and I joined the Baptist Church in Sweetwater and I had to quit drinking... Hasn't affected my brothers though."

Drinking Again

An Irishman had been drinking at a pub all night. The bartender finally said that the bar was closing. So the Irishman stood up to leave and fell flat on his face. He tried to stand one more time; same result. He figured he would crawl outside and get some fresh air and maybe that would sober him up. Once outside, he stood up and fell on his face again. So he decided to crawl the four blocks home. When he arrived at the door he stood up and fell flat on his face. He crawled through the door and into his bedroom. When he reached his bed, he tried one more time to stand up. This time he managed to pull himself upright, but he quickly fell right into the bed and was sound asleep as soon as his head hit the pillow.

He was awakened the next morning to his wife standing over him, shouting, "SO YOU'VE BEEN DRINKING AGAIN!"

Putting on an innocent look, and intent on bluffing it out he said, "What makes you say that?"

"The pub just called; you left your wheelchair there again."

Talk About Bad Luck

A pathetic guy is sitting at the bar just staring at his drink for half an hour when this big trouble-making truck driver steps next to him, grabs his drink and gulps it down in one swig. The poor little guy starts crying.

"Come on man, I was just giving you a hard time," says the truck driver. "I'll buy you another drink. I just can't stand to see a man crying."

"This is the worst day of my life," says the little guy between sobs. " I can't do anything right... I overslept and was late to an important meeting, so my boss fired me. When I went to the parking lot, I found my car was stolen and I have no insurance.

I grabbed a cab home but, after the cab left, I discovered my wallet was still in the cab. At home I found my wife in bed with the gardener. So I came to this bar trying to work up the courage to put an end to my life, and then you show up and drink the poison...

Top of the Empire State Building

Two men are sitting at the bar at the top of the Empire State Building drinking, when the first man turns to the other one and says: "You know, last week I discovered that if you jump from the top of this building, by the time you fall to the 10th floor, the wind around the building is so intense that it carries you around the building and back into the window."

The bartender just shakes his head in disapproval while wiping the bar, but says nothing.

The second guy says, "What? Are you insane? There's no way in heck that could happen!"

"No, it's true," said the first man, "let me prove it to you." He gets up from the bar, jumps over the balcony and plummets toward the street below. When he passes the 10th floor, the high wind whips him around the building and back into the 10th floor window and he takes the elevator back up to the bar. He meets the second man, who is astonished.

"You know, I saw that with my own eyes, but that must've been a one-time fluke. That was scientifically impossible!"

"No, I'll prove it again," says the first man as he jumps. Again, just as his body hurtles towards the street, the 10th floor wind gently carries him around the building and into the window. He takes the elevator back to the bar. Once upstairs, he successfully urges his dubious fellow drinker to try it.

"Well, what the heck," the second guy says, "I've seen that it works, so I'll try it!" He immediately jumps over the balcony - plunges downward -rapidly passes the 11th, 10th, 9th, 8th floors ...his body hits the sidewalk with a loud "splat."

Back upstairs, the bartender who had been silent the whole time turns to the first drinker, and shakes his head. He says, "You know, Superman, you're a real jerk when you're drunk."

Business and Law

Accountants and Engineers

Three engineers and three accountants are traveling by train to a conference. At the station, the three accountants each buy tickets and watch as the three engineers buy only a single ticket.

"How are three people going to travel on only one ticket?" asks an accountant.

"Watch and you'll see," answers an engineer.

They all board the train. The accountants take their respective seats but all three engineers cram into a restroom and close the door behind them. Shortly after the train has departed, the conductor comes around collecting tickets. He knocks on the restroom door and says, "Ticket, please." The door opens just a crack and a single arm emerges with a ticket in hand. The conductor takes it and moves on.

The accountants saw this and agreed it was quite a clever idea. So after the conference, the accountants decide to copy the engineers on the return trip and save some money (being clever with money, and all that). When they get to the station, they buy a single ticket for the return trip. To their astonishment, the engineers don't buy a ticket at all.

"How are you going to travel without a ticket?" says one perplexed accountant.

"Watch and you'll see," answers an engineer.

When they board the train the three accountants cram into a restroom and the three engineers cram into another one nearby. The train departs. Shortly afterward, one of the engineers leaves his restroom and walks over to the restroom where the accountants are hiding. He knocks on the door and says, "Ticket, please."

Blissful Words

A guy phones a law office and says: "I want to speak to my lawyer."

The receptionist replies "I'm sorry but he died last week."

The next day he phones again and asks the same question.

The receptionist replies "I told you yesterday, he died last week."

The next day the guy calls again and asks to speak to his lawyer.

By this time the receptionist is getting a little annoyed and says "I keep telling you that your lawyer died last week. Why do you keep calling?"

The guy says, "Because I just love hearing it."

Broke is Broke

A little old lady answered a knock on the door one day, only to be confronted by a well-dressed young man carrying a vacuum cleaner.

Good morning," said the young man. "If I could take a couple of minutes of your time, I would like to demonstrate the very latest in high-powered vacuum cleaners."

"Go away!" said the old lady. "I haven't got any money! I'M BROKE!!!" And she proceeded to close the door.

Quick as a flash, the young man wedged his foot in the door and pushed it wide open. "Don't be too hasty!" He said. "Not until you have at least seen my demonstration." And with that, he emptied a bucket of horse manure onto her hallway carpet.

"If this vacuum clear does not remove all traces of this horse manure from your carpet, Madam, I will personally eat the remainder." The old lady stepped back and said, "Well I hope you've got a good appetite, because they cut off my electricity this morning.

"When you go into court you are putting your fate into the hands of twelve people who weren't smart enough to get out of jury duty."   Norm Crosby

Clever Lawsuit

A man was sued by a woman for defamation of character. She charged that he had called her a pig. The man was found guilty and fined.

After the trial he asked the judge, "This means that I cannot call Mrs. Johnson a pig?" The judge said that was true.

"Does this mean I cannot call a pig Mrs. Johnson?" the man asked. The judge replied that he could indeed call a pig Mrs. Johnson with no fear of legal action.

The man looked directly at Mrs. Johnson and said, "Good afternoon, Mrs. Johnson."

"People who complain about taxes can be divided into two classes: men and women."   Unknown

CPA

A fellow learning to be a balloonist took his first solo flight. Unfortunately, the wind blew his balloon off course and he was forced to land. He was in a field close to a road but had no idea where he was. He saw a car coming along the road and waved at it. The driver stopped, got out, and the balloonist asked, "Can you please tell me where I am?"

"Yes, of course," replied the motorist. "You have just landed in your balloon and with this wind you have obviously been blown off course. You are in a field of John Dawson's farm, 4.5 miles from Lenox Township Center. John will be plowing the field next week and sowing wheat. There is a bull in the field with you. It is behind you and about to attack you."

At that moment the bull reached the balloonist and tossed him over the fence. Luckily, he was unhurt.

He got up, dusted himself off, and said to the motorist, "I see you've an accountant."

"Good grief," says the other man, "you're right. How did you know that?"

"I employ accountants," says the balloonist. "The information you gave me was detailed, precise, and accurate. Most of it was useless and it arrived far too late to be of any help."

Dead Horse Business Principles

The tribal wisdom of the Dakota Indians, passed on from one generation to the next, says that when you discover you are riding a dead horse, the best strategy is to dismount.

However, in modern business, because of the heavy investment factors to be taken into consideration, often other strategies have to be tried with dead horses, including the following:

1. Buying a stronger whip.
2. Changing riders.
3. Threatening the horse with termination.
4. Appointing a committee to study the horse.
5. Arranging to visit other sites to see how they ride dead horses.
6. Lowering the standards so that dead horses can be included.
7. Appointing an intervention team to reanimate the dead horse.
8. Creating a training session to increase the riders load share.
9. Reclassifying the dead horse as living-impaired.
10. Change the form so that it reads: "This horse is not dead."
11. Hire outside contractors to ride the dead horse.
12. Harness several dead horses together for increased speed.
13. Donate the dead horse to a recognized charity, thereby

deducting its full original cost.

14. Providing additional funding to increase the horse's performance.

15. Do a time management study to see if the lighter riders would improve productivity.

16. Purchase an after-market product to make dead horses run faster.

17. Declare that a dead horse has lower overhead and therefore performs better.

18. Form a quality focus group to find profitable uses for dead horses.

19. Rewrite the expected performance requirements for horses.

20. Promote the dead horse to a supervisory position.

Doing Nothing

A crow was sitting on a tree, doing nothing all day. A small rabbit saw the crow, and asked him, "Can I also sit like you and do nothing all day long?"

The crow answered: "Sure, why not."

So the rabbit sat on the ground below the crow and rested. All of a sudden, a fox appeared, jumped on the rabbit and ate it.

Management Lesson: To be sitting and doing nothing, you must be sitting very, very high up.

Heart Transplant

A man about to have a heart transplant was offered the choice of either a 26 year-old marathon runner's heart or the heart of a 62 year-old IRS agent. He picked the agent's heart because he said it had never been used.

Late Walmart Greeter

Charley, a new retiree greeter at Walmart, just couldn't seem to get to work on time. Every day he was 5, 10, sometimes 15 minutes late. But he was a good worker, really tidy, clean shaven, sharp minded and a real credit to the company and obviously demonstrating their "Older-Person-Friendly" policies.

One day the boss was in a real quandary about how to deal with it. Finally, he called him into the office for a talk.

"Charley, I have to tell you, I like your work ethic, you do a bang on job, but your being late so often is quite bothersome."

"Yes, I know, boss, and I am working on it."

"Well good, you are a team player. That's what I like to hear. It's odd though, your coming in late. I know you're retired from the Armed Forces. What did they say if you came in late there?"

"They usually said, 'Good morning, General. Tea or coffee this morning, sir?'"

Legal Observations

The Post Office just recalled their latest stamps. They had pictures of lawyers on them, and people couldn't figure out which side to spit on.

How can a pregnant woman tell that she's carrying a future lawyer? She has an uncontrollable craving for baloney.

How does an attorney sleep? First he lies on one side, and then he lies on the other.

How many lawyer jokes are there? Only three. The rest are true stories.

How many lawyers does it take to change a light bulb? How many can you afford?

How many lawyers does it take to screw in a light bulb? Three. One to climb the ladder, one to shake it, and one to sue the ladder company.

If a lawyer and an IRS agent were both drowning, and you could save only one of them, would you go to lunch or read the paper?

What did the lawyer name his daughter? Sue.

What do you call 25 skydiving lawyers? Skeet.

What do you call a lawyer gone bad? Senator.

What do you call a lawyer with an IQ of 50? Your Honor.

What do you throw to a drowning lawyer? His partners.

What does a lawyer use for birth control? His personality.

What happens when you cross a pig with a lawyer? Nothing. There are some things a pig won't do.

What's the difference between a lawyer and a vulture? The lawyer gets frequent flyer miles.

What's another difference between a lawyer and a vulture? Removable wing tips.

Life After Death

"Do you believe in life after death?" the boss asked one of his employees.

"Yes, sir," the new employee replied. "My whole family is made up of devout believers."

"Well, that explains it," the boss went on. "After you left early yesterday to
go to your grandmother's funeral, she stopped in to see you!"

My Daddy's Job

When I was a kid, my dad and I had a running joke. If anyone asked what he did for a living, I was to reply, "He's a sports mechanic. He fixes boxing matches and horse races."

Once, I answered a teacher this way. She flipped out and summoned my parents.

Dad calmed her down by explaining it was a joke.

"So what do you do?" she asked.

Dad, a sales rep for a pharmaceutical company, calmly said, "I sell drugs."

Say What?

A police officer pulled a guy over for speeding and had the following exchange:

Officer: May I see your driver's license?

Driver: I don't have one. I had it suspended when I got my 5th DUI.

Officer: May I see the owner's card for this vehicle?

Driver: It's not my car. I stole it.

Officer: The car is stolen?

Driver: That's right. But come to think of it, I think I saw the owner's card in the glove box when I was putting my gun in there.

Officer: There's a gun in the glove box?

Driver: Yes sir. That's where I put it after I shot and killed the woman who owns this car and stuffed her in the trunk.

Officer: There's a BODY in the TRUNK???

Driver: Yes sir.

Hearing this, the officer immediately called his captain. The car was quickly surrounded by police, and the captain approached the driver to handle the tense situation:

Captain: Sir, can I see your license?

Driver: Sure. Here it is.

It was valid.

Captain: Whose car is this?

Driver: It's mine officer. Here is the registration.

Captain: Could you slowly open your glove box so I can see if there's a gun in it?

Driver: Yessir, but there's no gun in it.

Sure enough, there was nothing in the glove box.

Captain: Would you mind opening your trunk? I was told there is a body in it.

Driver: No problem.

The trunk was opened; no body.

Captain: I don't understand it. The officer that stopped you said you told him you didn't have a license, had stolen the car, had a gun in the glove box, and that there was a dead body in the trunk.

Driver: Yeah. I bet he told you I was speeding, too.

Smart Jury

A defendant was on trial for murder. There was strong evidence indicating guilt, but there was no corpse. In the defense's closing statement, the lawyer, knowing that his client would probably be convicted, resorted to a trick.

"Ladies and gentlemen of the jury, I have a surprise for you all," the lawyer said as he looked at his watch. "Within one minute, the person presumed dead in this case will walk into this courtroom."

He looked toward the courtroom door. The jurors, somewhat stunned, all looked on eagerly. A minute passed. Nothing happened.

Finally, the lawyer said, "Actually, I made up the previous statement. But you all looked on with anticipation. I therefore put to you that you have a reasonable doubt in this case as to whether anyone was killed and insist that you return a verdict of not guilty."

The jury, clearly confused, retired to deliberate. A few minutes later, the jury returned and pronounced a verdict of guilty.

"But how?" inquired the lawyer. "You must have had some doubt; I saw all of you stare at the door."

The jury foreman replied: "Oh, we did look, but your client didn't."

The Lawyer and the Blond

A blonde and a lawyer are seated next to each other on a flight from LA to NY. The lawyer asks if she would like to play a fun game? The blonde, tired, just wants to take a nap, politely declines and rolls over to the window to catch a few winks. The lawyer persists and explains that the game is easy and a lot of fun. He explains, "I ask you a question, and if you don't know the answer, you pay me $5.00, and vise versa."

Again, she declines and tries to get some sleep. The lawyer, now agitated, says, "Okay, if you don't know the answer you pay me $5.00, and if I don't know the answer, I will pay you $500.00." This catches the blonde's attention and, figuring there will be no end to this torment unless she plays, agrees to the game.

The lawyer asks the first question. "What's the distance from the earth to the moon?" The blonde doesn't say a word, reaches into her purse, pulls out a $5.00 bill and hands it to the lawyer. Okay says the lawyer, your turn.

She asks the lawyer, "What goes up a hill with three legs and comes down with four legs?" The lawyer, puzzled, takes out his laptop computer and googles all his references, no answer. He taps into the library of congress, no answer. Frustrated, he texts all his friends and coworker, to no avail.

After an hour, he wakes the blonde, and hands her $500. The blonde says, "Thank you", and turns back to get some more sleep. The lawyer, who is more than a little miffed, wakes the blonde and asks, "Well, what's the answer?"

Without a word, the blonde reaches into her purse, hands the lawyer $5.00, and goes back to sleep.

And you thought blondes were supposed to be dumb.

The Mathematician, Economist and Tax Lawyer
A university committee was selecting a new dean. They had narrowed the candidates down to a mathematician, an economist and a tax lawyer.

Each was asked this question during their interview: "How much is two plus two?"

The mathematician answered immediately, "Four."

The economist thought for several minutes and finally answered, "Four, plus or minus one."

Finally, the tax lawyer stood up, peered around the room and motioned silently for the committee members to gather close to him. In a hushed, conspiratorial tone, he replied, "How much do you want it to be?"

Where There's Smoke There's Fire

A Charlotte, NC, lawyer purchased a box of very rare and expensive cigars: then insured them against fire among other things. Within a month having smoked his entire stockpile of these great cigars and without yet having made even his first premium payment on the policy, the lawyer filed a claim against the insurance company.

In his claim, the lawyer stated the cigars were lost "in a series of small fires."

The insurance company refused to pay, citing the obvious reason: that the man had consumed the cigars in the normal fashion.

The lawyer sued ... and won!

In delivering the ruling, the judge agreed with the insurance company that the claim was frivolous. The Judge stated, nevertheless, that the lawyer held a policy from the company in which it had warranted that the cigars were insurable and also guaranteed that it would insure them against fire, without defining what is considered to be unacceptable fire, and was obligated to pay the claim.

Rather than endure lengthy and costly appeal process, the insurance company accepted the ruling and paid $15,000 to the lawyer for his loss of the rare cigars lost in the "fires."

NOW FOR THE BEST PART...

After the lawyer cashed the check, the insurance company had him arrested on 24 counts of ARSON!!!! With his own insurance claim and testimony from the previous case being used against him, the lawyer was convicted of intentionally burning his insured property and was sentenced to 24 months in jail and a $24,000 fine.

Crime

A Blessing

A woman was getting a pie ready to put into the oven when the phone rang. It was the school nurse. Her son had come down with a high fever and would she come and take him home?

The mother calculated how long it would take to drive to school and back, and how long the pie should bake, and concluded there was enough time. Popping the pie in the oven, she left for school.

When she arrived, her son's fever was worse and the nurse urged her
to take him to the doctor.

Seeing her son like that -- his face flushed, his body trembling and dripping with perspiration -- frayed her, and she drove to the clinic as fast as she dared. She was frayed a bit more waiting for the doctor to emerge from the examining room, which he was doing now, walking toward her with a slip of paper in his hand.

"Get him to bed," he told her, handing her the prescription, "and start him on this right away."

By the time she got the boy home and in bed and headed out again for the shopping mall, she was not only frayed, but frazzled and frantic as well. She had forgotten about the pie in the oven. At the mall she found a pharmacy, got the prescription filled and rushed back to the car . . .

. . . which was locked.

Yes, there were her keys, hanging in the ignition switch, locked inside the car. She called home.

When her son finally answered, she blurted out, "I've locked the keys inside the car!" The boy was barely able to speak. In a hoarse voice

he whispered, "Get a wire coat hanger,
 Mom. You can get in with that." The phone went dead.

She began searching the mall for a wire coat hanger -- which turned but not to be easy. Wooden hangers and plastic hangers were there in abundance, but shops didn't use wire hangers anymore. After combing through a dozen stores, she found one that was behind the times just enough to use wire hangers.

Hurrying out of the mall, she allowed herself a smile of relief. As she was about to step off the curb, she halted. She stared at the wire coat hanger. "I don't know what to do with this!"

Then she remembered the pie in the oven. All the frustrations of the past hour collapsed on her and she began crying.

Then she prayed, "Dear Lord, my boy is sick and he needs this medicine and my pie is in the oven and the keys are locked in the car and Lord, I don't know what to do with this coat hanger. Dear Lord, send somebody who does know what do with it and I really need that person NOW, Lord. Amen."

She was wiping her eyes when a beat-up older car pulled up to the curb and stopped in front of her. A young man, twentyish-looking, in a T-shirt and ragged jeans, got out. The first thing she noticed about him was the long, stringy hair, and then the beard that hid everything south of his nose. He was coming her way.

When he drew near, she stepped in front of him and held out the wire coat hanger. "Young man," she said, "do you know how to get into a locked car with one of these?"

He gaped at her for a moment, then plucked the hanger from her hand. "Where's the car?"

Telling the story, she said she had never seen anything like it -- it was simply amazing how easily he got into her car. A quick look at the door and window, a couple of twists of the coat hanger and bam! Just like that, the door was open!

When she saw the door open, she threw her arms around him. "Oh," she said, "the Lord sent you! You're such a good boy. You must be a Christian!"

He stepped back and said, "No ma'am, I'm not a Christian, and

I'm not a good boy. I just got out of prison yesterday."

She jumped at him and she hugged him again - fiercely. "Praise the Lord!" she cried. "He sent me a professional!"

Mexican Bandit

A Mexican bandit made a specialty of crossing the Rio Grande from time to time and robbing banks in Texas. Finally, a reward was offered for his capture.

An enterprising Texas Ranger decided to track him down. After a lengthy search, he traced the bandit to his favorite cantina, sneaked up behind him, put his trusty six-shooter to the bandit's head and said, "You're under arrest. Tell me where you hid the loot or I'll blow your brains out."

But the bandit didn't speak English and the Ranger didn't speak Spanish! Fortunately, a bilingual lawyer was in the saloon and translated the Ranger's message.

The terrified bandit blurted out, in Spanish, that the loot was buried under the oak tree in back of the cantina.

"What did he say?" asked the Ranger.

The lawyer answered, "He said, 'Get lost, you turkey. You wouldn't dare shoot me.'"

The Burglar

A woman surprised a burglar in her kitchen. He was all loaded down with the things he was going to steal. She had no weapon and was all alone. The only thing that she could think to do was quote scripture. So, she holds up a hand and says: "ACTS 2:38!!!"

The burglar quakes in fear and then freezes to the point that she is able to get to the phone and call 911 for the cops. When the cops arrive, the burglar is still frozen in place. They are very much surprised that a woman alone with no weapon could do this.

One of them asked the lady: "How did you do this?"

The woman replied: "I quoted scripture."

The cop turned the burglar: "What was it about the Scripture that had such an effect on you?"

The burglar replied: "Scripture! What Scripture? I thought she said she had an axe and two 38's."

The Parrot and the Burglar

A burglar broke into a house one night. He shone his flashlight around, looking for valuables, and when he picked up a CD player to place into his sack, a strange, disembodied voice echoed from the dark saying, "Jesus is watching you."

He nearly jumped out of his skin, clicked his flashlight off and froze. When he heard nothing more after a bit, he shook his head, promised himself a long vacation after his next big score, then clicked the flashlight back on and began searching for more valuables.

Just as he pulled the stereo out so that he could disconnect the wires, clear as a bell he heard, "Jesus is watching you." Totally rattled, he shone his flashlight around frantically, looking for the source of the voice. Finally, in the corner of the room, his flashlight beam came to rest on a parrot.

"Did you say that"? he hissed at the parrot.

"Yes, the parrot confessed, then squawked, "I'm just trying to warn you."

The burglar relaxed. "Warn me, huh? Who do you think you are anyway?"

"Moses," replied the parrot.

"Moses", the burglar laughed. "What kind of people would name a parrot
"Moses?"

The parrot quickly answered, "The same kind of people that would name a
Rottweiler Jesus. Sic'em, Jesus!"

Education

An ode to English plurals
We'll begin with a box, and the plural is boxes, But the plural of ox
becomes oxen, not oxes.

One fowl is a goose, but two are called geese, Yet the plural of moose
should never be meese.

You may find a lone mouse or a nest full of mice, Yet the plural of house
is houses, not hice.

If the plural of man is always called men, Why shouldn't the plural of
pan be called pen?

If I speak of my foot and show you my feet, And I give you a boot, would
a pair be called beet?

If one is a tooth and a whole set are teeth, Why shouldn't the plural of
booth be called beeth?

Then one may be that, and three would be those,
Yet hat in the plural would never be hose, And the plural of cat is cats,
not cose.

We speak of a brother and also of brethren, But though we say mother,
we never say methren.

Then the masculine pronouns are he, his and him, But imagine the
feminine: she, shis and shim!

Let's face it - English is a crazy language. There is no egg in eggplant nor ham in hamburger; neither apple nor pine in pineapple. English muffins weren't invented in England .

We take English for granted, but if we explore its paradoxes, we find that quicksand can work slowly, boxing rings are square, and a guinea pig is neither from Guinea nor is it a pig.
And why is it that writers write but fingers don't fing, grocers don't groce and hammers don't ham?

Doesn't it seem crazy that you can make amends but not one amend.
If you have a bunch of odds and ends and get rid of all but one of them, what do you call it?

If teachers taught, why didn't preachers praught?
If a vegetarian eats vegetables, what does a humanitarian eat?

Sometimes I think all the folks who grew up speaking English should be committed to an asylum for the verbally insane.

In what other language do people recite at a play and play at a recital?

We ship by truck but send cargo by ship. We have noses that run and feet that smell.

We park in a driveway and drive in a parkway.
And how can a slim chance and a fat chance be the same,
while a wise man and a wise guy are opposites?

You have to marvel at the unique lunacy of a language in which your house can burn up as it burns down,
in which you fill in a form by filling it out, and in which an alarm goes off by going on.

And in closing, if Father is Pop, how come Mother's not Mop?

Exuberant Drummers

A wise old gentleman retired and purchased a modest home near a junior high school. He spent the first few weeks of his retirement in peace and contentment. Then a new school year began. The very next afternoon three young boys, full of youthful, after-school enthusiasm, came down his street, beating merrily on every trash can they encountered. The crashing percussion continued day after day, until finally the wise old man decided it was time to take some action.

The next afternoon, he walked out to meet the young percussionists as they banged their way down the street. Stopping them, he said, "You kids are a lot of fun. I like to see you express your exuberance like that. In fact, I used to do the same thing when I was your age. Will you do me a favor? I'll give you each a dollar if you'll promise to come around every day and do your thing."

The kids were elated and continued to do a bang-up job on the trash cans.

After a few days, the old-timer greeted the kids again, but this time he had a sad smile on his face. "This recession's really putting a big dent in my income," he told them. "From now on, I'll only be able to pay you 50 cents to beat on the cans."

The noisemakers were obviously displeased, but they accepted his offer and continued their afternoon ruckus.

A few days later, the wily retiree approached them again as they drummed their way down the street. "Look," he said, "I haven't received my Social Security check yet, so I'm not going to be able to give you more than 25 cents. Will that be okay?"

"A lousy quarter?" the drum leader exclaimed. "If you think we're going to waste our time, beating these cans around for a quarter, you're nuts! No way, mister. We quit!"

And the old man enjoyed peace and serenity for the rest of his days.

Finals

These four friends were so confident that the weekend before finals, they decided to go up to Dallas and party with some friends up there. They had a great time. However, after all the partying, they slept all day Sunday and didn't make it back to Austin until early Monday morning. Rather than taking the final then, they decided to find their professor after the final and explain to him why they missed it.

They explained that they had gone to Dallas for the weekend with the plan to come back and study but, unfortunately, they had a flat tire on the way back, didn't have a spare, and couldn't get help for a long time. As a result, they missed the final. The Professor thought it over and then agreed they could make up the final the following day.

The guys were elated and relieved. They studied that night and went in the next day at the time the professor had told them. He placed them in separate rooms and handed each of them a test booklet, and told them to begin.

They looked at the first problem, worth 5 points. It was something simple about free radical formation. "Cool," they thought at the same time, each one in his separate room. "This is going to be easy." Each finished the problem and then turned the page.

On the second page was written: (For 95 points): Which tire?

Goats and School

A group of Montana high school students played a prank: they let three goats loose in the school building. But before they let them go, they painted numbers on the sides of the goats: 1, 2 and 4. The best part of the prank was when, after they had rounded up the three goats, the school administrators spent the rest of the day looking for goat #3.

Quick Guide for English Teachers

1. Verbs HAS to agree with their subjects.
2. Prepositions are not words to end sentences with.
3. And don't start a sentence with a conjunction.
4. It is wrong to ever split an infinitive.
5. Avoid clichés like the plague. (They're old hat)
6. Also, always avoid annoying alliteration.
7. Be more or less specific.
8. Parenthetical remarks (however relevant) are (usually) unnecessary.
9. Also, too, never, ever use repetitive redundancies.
10. No sentence fragments.
11. Contractions aren't necessary and shouldn't be used.
12. Foreign words and phrases are not apropos.
13. Do not be redundant; do not use more words than necessary; it's highly superfluous.
14. One should NEVER generalize.
15. Comparisons are as bad as clichés.
16. Eschew ampersands & abbreviations, etc.
17. One-word sentences? Eliminate.
18. Analogies in writing are like feathers on a snake.
19. The passive voice is to be ignored.
20. Eliminate commas, that are, not necessary. Parenthetical words however should be enclosed in commas.
21. Never use a big word when a diminutive one would suffice.
22. Use words correctly, irregardless of how others use them.
23. Understatement is always the absolute best way to put forth earth shaking ideas.
24. Eliminate quotations. As Ralph Waldo Emerson said, "I hate quotations. Tell me what you know."
25. If you've heard it once, you've heard it a thousand times: Resist hyperbole; not one writer in a million can use it correctly.
26. Puns are for children, not groan readers.

Teacher?

TEACHER: Maria, go to the map and find North America .
MARIA: Here it is.
TEACHER: Correct. Now class, who discovered America ?
CLASS: Maria.

TEACHER: John, why are you doing your math multiplication on the floor?
JOHN: You told me to do it without using tables.

TEACHER: Glenn, how do you spell 'crocodile?'
GLENN: K-R-O-K-O-D-I-A-L'
TEACHER: No, that's wrong
GLENN: Maybe it is wrong, but you asked me how I spell it.

TEACHER: Donald, what is the chemical formula for water?
DONALD: H I J K L M N O.
TEACHER: What are you talking about?
DONALD: Yesterday you said it's H to O.

TEACHER: Winnie, name one important thing we have today that we didn't have ten years ago.
WINNIE: Me!

TEACHER: Glen, why do you always get so dirty?
GLEN: Well, I'm a lot closer to the ground than you are.

TEACHER: Millie, give me a sentence starting with ' I. '
MILLIE: I is..
TEACHER: No, Millie..... Always say, 'I am.'
MILLIE: All right... 'I am the ninth letter of the alphabet.'

TEACHER: George Washington not only chopped down his father's cherry tree, but also admitted it. Now, Louie, do you know why his father didn't punish him?
LOUIS: Because George still had the axe in his hand..

TEACHER: Now, Simon, tell me frankly, do you say prayers before eating?

SIMON: No sir, I don't have to, my Mom is a good cook.

TEACHER: Clyde , your composition on 'My Dog' is exactly the same as your brother's. Did you copy his?
CLYDE : No, sir. It's the same dog.

TEACHER: Harold, what do you call a person who keeps on talking when people are no longer interested?
HAROLD: A teacher

Teacher's Presents

It was the end of the school year, and a kindergarten teacher was receiving gifts from her pupils. The florist's son handed her a gift. She shook it, held it overhead and said, "I bet I know what it is. Flowers."

That's right!" the boy said, "But how did you know?"

"Oh, just a wild guess," the teacher said.

The next student was the candy store owner's daughter. The teacher held her gift box overhead, shook it, and said, "I bet I can guess what it is. A box of chocolates."

That's right Miss Jones, but how did you know?" asked the girl.

"Oh, just a wild guess," said the teacher.

The next gift was from the son of the liquor store owner. The teacher started to hold his package overhead, but noticed it was leaking. She touched a drop of the liquid with her finger and tasted it. "Is it wine?" she asked.

"No," the boy replied, with some excitement.

The teacher repeated the process, tasting a larger drop of the leakage. "Is it champagne?" she asked.

"No," the boy replied, with more excitement.

Miss Jones took one more big taste before declaring, "I give up, what is it?"

With great glee, the boy replied, "It's a puppy!"

The Importance of Correct Punctuation

Dear John

I want a man who knows what love is all about. You are generous, kind, thoughtful. People who are not like you admit to being useless and inferior. You have ruined me for other men. I yearn for you. I have no feelings whatsoever when we're apart. I can be forever happy—will you let me be yours?

Gloria

Dear John

I want a man who knows what love is. All about you are generous, kind, thoughtful people, who are not like you. Admit to being useless and inferior. You have ruined me. For other men, I yearn. For you, I have no feelings whatsoever. When we're apart, I can be forever happy. Will you let me be?

Yours,

Gloria

Eyes of a Child

Call the Fire Department

The boss of a big company needed to call one of his employees about an urgent problem that had come up after that employee had left for the day. He dialed the employee's home phone number and was greeted with a child's whispered, "Hello?"

The boss asked, "Is your Daddy home?"

"Yes," whispered the small voice.

"May I talk with him?" the man asked.

To his surprise, the small voice whispered, "No."

"Is your Mommy there?"

"Yes."

"May I talk with her?"

"No."

"Is there any one there besides you?" the boss asked the child.

"Yes," whispered the child. "A policeman."

Wondering what a cop would be doing at his employee's home, the boss asked, "May I speak with the policeman?"

"No, he's busy," whispered the child.

"Busy doing what?"

"Talking to Daddy and Mommy and the fireman," came the whispered answer.

Growing worried as he heard what sounded like a helicopter through the earpiece on the phone, the boss asked, "What is that noise?"

"A hello-copper," answered the whispering voice.

"What is going ON there?" asked the boss, now alarmed.

In an awed whisper the child answered, "The search team just landed the hello-copper."

Now really alarmed, the boss asked, "Why are THEY there?"

Still whispering, the young voice replied along with a muffled giggle, "They're looking for me!"

Cat Burial

Little Tim was in the garden filling in a hole when his neighbor peered over the fence. Interested in what the youngster was up to, he politely asked, "What are you doing there, Tim?"

"My cat died," replied Tim tearfully, without looking up, "and I've just buried her."

The neighbor was concerned, "That's an awfully big hole for a cat, isn't it?

Tim patted down the last heap of earth then replied, "That's because she's inside your Rottweiler."

It's up to You

A mother was preparing pancakes for her sons, Kevin, 5, and Ryan, 3. The boys began to argue over who would get the first pancake. Their mother saw the opportunity for a moral lesson.

If Jesus were sitting here, He would say, "Let my brother have the first pancake. I can wait."

Kevin turned to his younger brother and said, "Ryan, you be Jesus.

Food

Science: Bread is Dangerous

1. More than 98 percent of convicted felons are bread users.

2. Fully HALF of all children who grow up in bread- consuming households score below average on standardized tests.

3. In the 18th century, when virtually all bread was baked in the home, the average life expectancy was less than 50 years; infant mortality rates were unacceptably high; many women died in childbirth; and diseases such as typhoid, yellow fever, and influenza ravaged whole nations.

4. More than 90 percent of violent crimes are committed within 24 hours of eating bread.

5. Bread has been proven to be addictive. Subjects deprived of bread and given only water to eat, begged for bread after as little as two days.

6. Bread is often a "gateway" food item, leading the user to "harder" items such as butter, jelly, peanut butter, and even cream cheese.

7. Bread has been proven to absorb water. Since the human body is more than 90 percent water, it follows that eating bread could lead to your body being taken over by this absorptive

food product, turning you into a soggy, gooey, bread-pudding person.

8. Newborn babies can choke on bread.

9. Bread is baked at temperatures as high as 450 degrees Fahrenheit! That kind of heat can kill an adult in less than two minutes.

10. Most American bread eaters are utterly unable to distinguish between significant scientific fact and meaningless statistical babbling.

Chicken, Anyone?

One day a State Trooper was pulling off an expressway near Chicago. When he turned onto the street at the end of the ramp, he noticed someone at a chicken place getting into his car. The driver placed the bucket of chicken on top of his car, got in and drove off with the bucket still on top of his car.

So the trooper decides to pull him over and perform a community service by giving the driver his chicken. He pulled him over, walked up to the car, pulled the bucket off the roof and offered it to the driver.

The driver looks at the trooper and said, "No thanks, I just bought one."

Chocolate Rules (Rules For Chocolate Lovers)
- If you've got melted chocolate all over your hands, you're eating it too slowly.
- Chocolate covered raisins, cherries, orange slices & strawberries all count as fruit.

- Problem: How to get 2 pounds of chocolate home from the store in hot car. Solution: Eat it in the parking lot.
- Diet tip: Eat a chocolate bar before each meal. It takes the edge off your appetite and you'll eat less.
- If you can't eat all your chocolate, it will keep in the freezer. But if you can't eat all your chocolate, what is wrong with you?
- If calories are an issue with you, store the chocolate on top of the fridge. Calories are afraid of heights, and they will jump out of the chocolate to protect themselves.
- Equal amounts of dark chocolate and white chocolate make a balanced diet.
- Money talks. Chocolate sings.
- Question: Why is there no such organization as Chocoholics Anonymous? Answer: Because no one wants to quit.
- Put "eat chocolate" at the top of your list of things to do today. That way, at least you'll get one thing done.

Clean Glass

Waiter: Tea or coffee, gentlemen?

1st customer: I'll have tea.

2nd customer: Me, too. And be sure the glass is clean!

(Waiter exits, returns)

Waiter: Two teas. Which one asked for the clean glass?

Diet Solution

A woman in a diet club was lamenting that she had gained weight. She'd made her family's favorite cake over the weekend, she reported, and they'd eaten half of it at dinner.

Her husband teased her and said she would never be able to stay away from the other half until dinner the next night

The next day, she said, she kept staring at the other half, until finally she cut a thin slice for herself. One slice led to another, and soon the whole cake was gone. The woman went on to tell us how upset she was with her lack of willpower, and how she knew her husband would rub it in.

Everyone commiserated; until someone asked what her husband said when he found out. She smiled. "He never found out. I made another cake and ate half!"

Dynamite Diet

A tough old Texas cowboy counseled his grandson, "The secret of living a long life is to eat oatmeal every morning with a pinch of gunpowder sprinkled on it."

The grandson followed his grandfather's advice religiously and lived to the ripe old age of 103. When he died, he left 14 children, 30 grandchildren, 45 great grandchildren, 25 great-great grandchildren…and a 15 foot hole where the crematorium used to be.

Elephant Stew Recipe

2 Rabbits (Optional)

1 Elephant, Medium Size

Salt & Pepper to taste

Brown Gravy

Cut elephant into small bite-sized pieces. This should take about two months. Add enough brown gravy to cover. Cook over kerosene fire for about four weeks at 465 degrees. This will serve 3800 people. If more are expected, two rabbits may be added, but do this only if necessary, as some people do not like to find a hare in their stew.

"Red meat is NOT bad for you. Now, blue-green meat, that's REALLY
BAD for you."   Tommy Smothers

Meatloaf Dinner

A recent bride called her mother one evening in tears. "Oh,
Mom, I tried to make Grandmother's meat loaf for dinner tonight, and
it's just awful! I followed the recipe exactly, and I know I have the recipe
right because it's the one you gave me. But it just didn't come out right,
and I'm so upset. I wanted this to be so special for George because he
loves meat loaf. What could have gone wrong?"

Her mother replied soothingly, "Well, dear, let's go through the
recipe. You read it out loud and tell me exactly what you did at each
step, and together we'll figure it out."

"OK," the bride sniffled. "Well, it starts out, ' Take fifty cents
worth of ground beef '..."

!!!Merry Christmas!!!
'Twas the night after Christmas, But I just couldn't sleep.
 I tried counting backwards, I tried counting sheep
The leftovers beckoned The dark meat and white,
But I fought the temptation with all of my might.

Tossing and turning with anticipation,
The thought of a snack became infatuation!
So I raced to the kitchen, Flung open the door,
And gazed at the fridge full of goodies galore.

I gobbled up turkey and buttered potatoes,
Pickles and carrots, beans and tomatoes.
I felt myself swelling so plump and so round,
Till all of a sudden, I rose off the ground!!

I crashed through the ceiling, floated into the sky
 With a mouthful of pudding and a handful of pie,
But I managed to yell as I soared past the trees ...

Happy Eating to All,
Pass the Cranberries Please!!

Pillsbury Doughboy Dead

Veteran Pillsbury spokesman Pop N. Fresh died Wednesday of a severe yeast infection. He was 71. He was buried Friday in one of the biggest funerals in years. Dozens of celebrities turned out including Mrs. Butterworth, the California Raisins, Hungry Jack, Betty Crocker, and the Hostess Twinkies.

The graveside was piled high with flours, as longtime friend Aunt Jemima delivered the eulogy, describing Fresh as a man who "never knew how much he was kneaded".

Fresh rose quickly in show business, but his later life was filled with turnovers. He was not considered a smart cookie, and wasted much of his dough on half-baked schemes. Still, even as a crusty old man, he was a roll model to millions.

Fresh is survived by his second wife. They had two children, and ... one in the oven.

The Three Little Pigs

There were three little pigs that went to a restaurant for dinner. The
waiter came to the table and asked if they would like something to drink.

The first piggy said, "I would like a Dr. Pepper."
The second piggy said, "I would like a glass of tea."

The third piggy said, "I would like a glass of water."

When the waiter brought the drinks, he asked if they were ready to order.

The first piggy said he would like a Hamburger."

The second piggy said, "I would like a Steak."

The third piggy said, "I would like a glass of water."

When the piggies were finished eating, the waiter asked if they would
like some dessert.

The first piggy said, "I would like a hot fudge sundae."

The second piggy said, "I would like a banana split."

The third piggy said, "I would like a glass of water."

When the piggies were finished with dessert, the waiter brought their check.

Before he left the table, he asked the third little piggy why he only ordered water.

The third piggy said, "Well, someone has to go 'Wee wee wee all the way home."

Growing Older

Eternal Worrier

The ninety-five year old woman at the nursing home received a visit from one of her fellow church members.

"How are you feeling?" the visitor asked.

"Oh," said the lady, "I'm just worried sick!"

"What are you worried about, dear?" her friend asked. "You look like you're in good health. They are taking care of you, aren't they?"

"Yes, they are taking very good care of me."

"Are you in any pain?" she asked.

"No, I have never had a pain in my life."

"Well, what are you worried about?" her friend asked again.

The lady leaned back in her rocking chair and slowly explained her major worry. "Every close friend I ever had has already died and gone on to heaven. I'm afraid they're all wondering where I went."

Aging: Eventually you will reach a point when you stop lying about your age and start bragging about it.

Some people try to turn back their odometers. Not me, I want people to know "why" I look this way. I've traveled a long way and some of the roads weren't paved.

Big Alarm

One dark night outside a small town, a fire started inside the local chemical plant and before you could snap your fingers it exploded into flames and the alarm went out to the volunteer fire departments from miles around.

When the volunteer firefighters appeared on the scene, the chemical company president rushed to the fire chief and said, "All of our secret formulas are in the vault in the center of the plant. They must be saved. I will give $50,000 to the engine company that brings them out intact."

The fire chief ordered his men to strengthen their attack on the blaze. After two hours of fighting the fire another fire department was called in and the president of the chemical company offered $100,000 to the firefighters who could bring out the company's secret files. From the distance, a long siren was heard as another fire truck came into sight. It was the local volunteer fire company composed entirely of men over the age of 65. To everyone's amazement, the little fire engine raced passed everyone and drove straight into the middle of the inferno.

Outside the other firemen watched as the old timers jumped off their rig and began to fight the fire with a performance and effort never seen before. Within a short time, the old timers had extinguished the fire and saved the secret formulas. The grateful chemical company president joyfully announced that for such a super-human feat he was upping the reward to $200,000, and walked over to personally thank each of the brave, though elderly, fire fighters.

The local TV news reporters rushed in after capturing the event on film asking. "What are you going to do with all that money?"

Well," said the 70-year-old fire chief, "the first thing we are going to do is fix the brakes on the truck."

Clear Enough

Morris, an 82 year- old man, went to the doctor to get a physical. A few days later, the doctor saw Morris walking down the street with a gorgeous young woman in his arm.

A couple of days later, the doctor spoke to Morris and said, "You're really doing great, aren't you?"

Morris replied, "Just doing what you said, Doc. Gat a hot mama and be cheerful."

What I said was, "You've got a heart murmur; be careful!"

Important Prescription

A distraught senior citizen phoned her doctor's office. "Is it true," she wanted to know, "that the medication you prescribed has to be taken for the rest of my life?"

"Yes, I'm afraid so," the doctor told her.

There was a moment of silence before the senior lady replied, "I'm wondering, then, just how serious is my condition because this prescription is marked 'NO REFILLS'."

Old age is when former classmates are so gray and wrinkled and bald, they don't recognize you.

If you don't learn to laugh at trouble, you won't have anything to laugh at when you are old.

First you forget names, then you forget faces. Then you forget to pull up your zipper. It's worse when you forget to pull it down...

My Forgetter
My forgetter's getting better
But my rememberer is broke.
To you that may seem funny but,
to me, that is no joke.

For when I'm "here" I'm wondering
If I really should be "there."
And, when I try to think it through,
I haven't got a prayer!

Oft times I walk into a room,
Say "what am I here for?"
I wrack my brain, but all in vain;
A zero, is my score.

At times I put something away
Where it is safe, but, Gee!
The person it is safest from
Is, generally, me!

When shopping I may see someone,
Say "Hi" and have a chat,
Then, when the person walks away
I ask myself "who's that?"

Yes, my forgetter's getting better
While my rememberer is broke,
And it's driving me plumb crazy

And that isn't any joke.

Author unknown (or maybe forgotten)

New Hearing Aid

An elderly gentleman had serious hearing problems for a number of years. He went to the doctor and the doctor was able to have him fitted for a set of hearing aids that allowed the gentleman to hear 100%.

The elderly gentleman went back in a month to the doctor and the doctor said, "Your hearing is perfect. Your family must be really pleased that you can hear again."

The gentleman replied, "Oh, I haven't told my family yet. I just sit around and listen to the conversations. I've changed my will three times!"

Perks of Getting Older

1. Kidnappers are not very interested in you.
2. In a hostage situation you are likely to be released first.
3. No one expects you to run--anywhere.
4. People call at 9 pm and ask, " Did I wake you?"
5. People no longer view you as a hypochondriac.
6. There is nothing left to learn the hard way.
7. Things you buy now won't wear out.
8. You can eat dinner at 4 pm.
9. You can live without sex but not your glasses.
10. You enjoy hearing about other people's operations.
11. You get into heated arguments about pension plans.
12. You no longer think of speed limits as a challenge.
13. You quit trying to hold your stomach in no matter who walks into the room.
14. You sing along with elevator music.
15. Your eyes won't get much worse.

16. Your investment in health insurance is finally beginning to pay off.

17. Your joints are more accurate meteorologists than the national weather service.

18. Your secrets are safe with your friends because they can't remember them either.

19. Your supply of brain cells is finally down to manageable size.

Proud Grandmother

An elderly, wealthy woman in Florida was boring fellow beachcombers as she bragged on and on about her two remarkable grandchildren. Unable to stand it any longer, a fellow sunbather interrupted her.

"Tell me, how old are your grandsons?"

The grandmother gave a grateful smile and replied, "The doctor is four and the lawyer is six..."

Speeding Senior

A Florida senior citizen drove his brand new Corvette convertible out of the dealership. Taking off down the road, he pushed it to 80 mph, Enjoying the wind blowing through what little hair he had left. "Amazing," he thought as he flew down I-75, pushing the pedal even more. Looking in his rear view mirror, he saw a Florida state trooper, blue lights flashing and siren blaring. He floored it to 100 mph, then 110, then 120.

Suddenly he thought, "What am I doing? I'm too old for this!" and pulled over to await the trooper's arrival.

Pulling in behind him, the trooper got out of his vehicle and walked up to the Corvette. He looked at his watch, then said, "Sir, my shift ends in 30 minutes. Today is Friday. If you can give me a new reason for speeding--a reason I've never before heard -- I'll let you go."

The old gentleman paused then said: "Three years ago, my wife ran off with a Florida state trooper. I thought you were bringing her back.

Have a good day, sir," replied the trooper.

The Old Dentist

While waiting in the reception room for my first appointment with a new dentist I noticed his diploma, which bore his full name. Suddenly, I remembered that a tall, handsome boy with the same name had been in my high school class some 45 years ago. Upon seeing him, however, I quickly discarded any thought that he might have been my classmate. This balding, gray-haired man with the deeply lined face was much too old to have gone to school with me.

After he examined my teeth, I asked him if he had attended the local high school.

"Yes," he replied. "When did you graduate?" I asked. He answered, "1957."

"Why, you were in my class!" I exclaimed.

He looked at me closely and then asked, "What did you teach?"

Walmart Adventures

Two old guys are pushing their carts around Wal-Mart when they collide. The first old guy says to the second guy, "Sorry about that. I'm looking for my wife, and I guess I wasn't paying attention to where I was going."

The second old guy says, "That's OK, It's a coincidence. I'm looking for my wife, too. I can't find her and I'm getting a little desperate."

The first old guy says, "Well, maybe I can help you find her. What does she look like?"

The second old guy says: "Well, she is 27 years old, tall, with red hair, blue eyes, long legs, and is wearing short shorts. What does your wife look like?"

To which the first old guy says, "Doesn't matter, --- let's look for yours."

Write it Down!

An elderly husband and wife went to the doctor, concerned because of increased forgetfulness that they might be developing Alzheimer's. After complete examinations, the doctor told the couple that it was only their older age affecting their memory. He suggested they simply start writing things down to help them remember. They went home and continued their daily routine. That evening, while watching TV, the husband started to the kitchen to get something to eat. The wife asked him to bring her a bowl of ice cream.

He turned to go and she reminded him that he should write it down as the doctor instructed or he would forget it. He said he could remember a bowl of ice cream.

She then said she wanted strawberries on the ice cream. She again told him to write this down or he'd forget it.

He was agitated, insisting he could remember a bowl of ice cream with strawberries.

Finally, she said she'd like to have whipped cream on top. She insisted again that he should write it all down. He angrily stormed into the kitchen.

He returned 20 minutes later and handed her a plate of bacon and eggs.

She looked at the plate in disgust and said, "See, I told you to write it down. You forgot my toast!"

You've Got Mail

Working at the post office, I'm used to dealing with a moody public. So, when one irate customer stormed my desk, I responded in my calmest voice, "What's the trouble?"

"I went out this morning," she began, "and when I came home, I found a card saying the mailman tried to deliver a package, but no one was home. I'll have you know, my husband was in all morning! He never heard a thing!"

After apologizing, I got her parcel.

"Oh good!" she gushed. "We've been waiting for this for ages!"

"What is it?" I asked.

"My husband's new hearing aid."

"Next!"

Great Country

Bungee in Mexico

Ed and Bill moved to Mexico to open a bungee-jumping business. On the first day, they offered a demonstration to spur the locals to open their wallets. Bill attached the cord to his ankle and dove off the tower. He soared toward the crowd and then sprang back up. When Bill got near the top, Ed noticed his friend's clothes were torn. The next time he popped up, Bill had a few small scrapes, and the third time he looked bruised. Finally, he came to a stop and staggered up the ladder.

"What happened to you?" Ed asked.

"I don't know," Bill answered. "What's a pinata?.

Circle Flies

After pulling a farmer over for speeding, a state trooper started to lecture him about his speed, pompously implying that the farmer didn't know any better and trying to make him feel as uncomfortable as possible. He finally started writing out the ticket, but had to keep swatting at some flies buzzing around his head.

The farmer said, "Having some problems with circle flies there are ya?"

The trooper paused to take another swat and said, "Well, yes, if that's what they are. I've never heard of circle flies."

The farmer was pleased to enlighten the cop. "Circle flies are common on farms. They're called circle flies because you almost always find them circling the back end of a horse."

The trooper continues writing for a moment, then says," Hey, are you trying to call me a horse's behind?"

"Oh no, officer, "The farmer replies. "I have too much respect for law enforcement and police officers for that."

"That's a good thing," the officer says rudely, then goes back to writing the ticket.

After a long pause, the farmer added, "Hard to fool them flies, though."

Dead Dog

Deep in the woods of Tennessee on a country road, a speeder hit and killed a dog. The dog's owner stood nearby, a gun in his hand.

The speeder looks at the owner sheepishly and says, "Looks as if I killed your dog."

"Sure does."

"I'm sorry. Was it a valuable dog?"

"I wouldn't say that."

"Well, suppose I gave you a hundred dollars. Would that be enough?"

"Well, I don't know."

"Two hundred dollars. That should do it."

"Sounds good."

The speeder reached into his pocket and came up with the money. Pressing it into the man's hand, he said, "I'm sorry I spoiled your plans to go hunting."

"I wasn't going hunting. I was heading out to the woods to shoot that mangy dog."

Froze Over

Boudreaux died and went to hell. He was out at the edge of hell just partying and having the best time.

Satan went over there to see what all the commotion was about. "Why are you having so much fun? Aren't you hot?"

"Oh, it's no worse than Louisiana in June" he said.

So Satan went back to his minions and instructed them to turn up the heat. Next time he checked Boudreaux was still over there partying and having the best time.

Again Satan said, "Aren't you hot?"

"Oh, no, it's no worse than Louisiana in August."

Next thin you know it got cold, really cold. And Boudreaux was really whooping it up then.

"What's going on? Satan asked"

Boudreaux let out a howl of celebration. "The Saints won the Super Bowl!"

Halo Statue

A Mexican man becomes an instant millionaire after winning the lottery. With his newfound wealth, he decides on exactly what he will buy. He buys a 20 acre plot of land in Mexico and hires an architect. He tells the architect, "I want mi casa to be built right there, with big columns in front, and a marble foyer, and at the end of the hall I want a halo statue."

The architect, excited about making mega bucks off this man, jots down exactly what the Mexican wants," I'll do it sir, I'll make this a fine house for you!"

All the plans are made and the architect starts construction. He searches six different countries to find exquisite columns for the front of the house and has marble shipped in from France to line the foyer. The only problem he has is that he cannot locate a halo statue. Knowing that religious symbols are important to many Mexicans, he continues to search high and low for month after month. The house is finally complete, but alas, the architect was never able to locate a halo statue.

Swallowing his pride for not being able to complete the order, he takes the Mexican to see his new home.

"Si Senor!" exclaims the Mexican. "You got da columns in front of mi casa!"

The architect smiles.

They enter the house and the Mexican notices the marble floor. "Wonderful! I love mi new marble floor Senor!" states the Mexican.

As he wanders down the hall. He reaches the end of the hall and looks puzzled. "Senor? Where is my halo statue?" asks the Mexican.

"Well, sir, I'm afraid to have to tell you this, but I searched high and low and just could not for the life of me figure out what a halo statue is, much less find one for you anywhere," says the architect, hanging his head in shame.

"What? You don't know what a halo statue is?"

"No, sir, I'm sorry, I do not know," replies the architect.

"You know," says the Mexican, "it's that thing that goes 'ringy dingy' and you pick it up and say, "halo?... statue?"

Hans Olafsen's Laundry

This guy is walking through Chinatown. He is fascinated with all the Chinese Restaurants, the Chinese shops, the Chinese signs and banners on the buildings. He turns a corner and sees a building with a sign "Hans Olafsen's Laundry". "Hans Olafsen?" he thinks. "How in the world does that fit in here?"

So, he walks into the shop and sees an old Chinese gentleman sitting in the corner. The visitor asks, "How in the world did this place get a name like Hans Olafsen's Laundry?"

The old man answers, "Is name of owner."

The visitor asks, "Well, where's the owner?"

"I am he," answers the old man.

"You? How did you ever get a name like Hans Olafsen?"

The old man replies, "Many years ago when I come to this country, I was standing in line at Documentation Center. Man in front of me was big blonde Swede. Lady look at him and go "What your name? He say Hans Olafsen. She look at me... What your name?

I say Sam Ting.

Old Technology

After having dug to a depth of 10 feet last year, New York scientists found traces of copper wire dating back 100 years and came to the conclusion that their ancestors already had a telephone network more than 100 years ago."

Not to be outdone by the New Yorkers in the weeks that followed, an archaeologist in California dug to a depth of 20 feet and shortly afterwards, headlines in the LA Times newspaper read: "California archaeologists have found traces of 200-year-old copper wire and have concluded that their ancestors already had an advanced high-tech
communications network a hundred years earlier than the New Yorkers."

One week later, The Leesburg News, a local newspaper in Central Florida, reported the following: "After digging as deep as 30 feet in his pasture, near Travelers Rest, Lake County Florida, Bubba Mitchell, a self-taught archaeologist, reported that he found absolutely nothing. Bubba has, therefore, concluded that 300 years ago, Central Florida had already gone wireless."

Thank Goodness for Bubba. Who said local Floridians were hicks?

Raining in Seattle

A newcomer to Seattle arrived on a rainy day. He got up the next day and it was raining. It also rained the day after that, and the day after that. He went out to lunch and saw a young kid and, out of despair, asked, "Hey, kid, does it ever stop raining around here?"

"How should I know?" the youngster said. "I'm only 6."

Visiting Texas

Boudreaux and Thibodeaux are from Louisiana visiting a relative at the Huntsville, Texas prison. Walking along Sam Houston Street, they see a sign which reads: 'Suits $5.00 each, shirts $2.00 each, trousers $2.50 per pair.

Boudreaux says to his pal, "Hey Thib, LOOK! We could buy a whole lot of those, and when we get back to Lafayette, we could make a fortune. Now when we go into the shop, you be quiet, okay? Just let me do all the talkin' cause if they hear our Cajun accent they might not serve us. I'll speak in my best Texas drawl." They go in and Boudreaux orders 50 suits at 5.00 each, 100 shirts at 2.00 each and 50 pairs of trousers at 2.50 each.

The owner of the shop says, "You're from Louisiana, aren't you?"

"Oh, ... yes," says a surprised Boudreaux. "How come you know dat?

"The owner says, "Cause this is a dry-cleaners."

Why Are We Still There? (WAWST?)

We occupied this land, which we had to take by force, but it causes us nothing but trouble. Why are we still there?

Many of our children go there and never come back. Why are we still there?

Their government is unstable, and until recently they've had loopy leadership. WAWST?

Many of their people are uncivilized. WAWST?

The place is subject to natural disasters, which we are supposed to bail them out of. WAWST?

There are more than 1000 religious sects, which we do not understand. WAWST?

Their folkways, foods and fads are unfathomable to ordinary Americans. WAWST?

We can't even secure the borders. WAWST?

They are billions of dollars in debt and it will cost billions more to rebuild, which we can't afford. Why are we still there?

The answer is clear..
We must pull out of California.

Things I Have Learned from Watching Movies

...All telephone numbers in America begin with the digits 555.

...If being chased through town, you can usually take cover in a passing St. Patrick's Day parade - at any time of the year.

...All beds have special L-shaped cover sheets which reach up to the armpit level on a woman but only to waist level on the man lying beside her.

...All grocery shopping bags contain at least one stick of French Bread.

...It's easy for anyone to land a plane providing there is someone in the control tower to talk you down.

...Once applied, lipstick will never rub off - even while scuba diving.

...The ventilation system of any building is the perfect hiding place. No one will ever think of looking for you in there and you can travel to any other part of the building you want without difficulty.

...If you need to reload your gun, you will always have more ammunition - even if you haven't been carrying any before now.

...You're very likely to survive any battle in any war unless you make the mistake of showing someone a picture of your sweetheart back home.

...Should you wish to pass yourself off as a German officer, it will not be necessary to speak the language. A German accent will do.

...The Eiffel Tower can be seen from any window in Paris.

...A man will show no pain while taking the most ferocious beating but will wince when a woman tries to clean his wounds.

...When paying for a taxi, don't look at your wallet as you take out a bill - just grab one at random and hand it over. It will always be the exact fare.

...Kitchens don't have light switches. When entering a kitchen at night, you should open the fridge door and use that light instead.

...Mothers routinely cook eggs, bacon and waffles for their family every morning even though their husband and children never have time to eat it.

...Cars that crash will almost always burst into flames.

...The Chief of Police will always suspend his star detective - or give him 48 hours to finish the job.

...A single match will be sufficient to light up a room the size of RFK Stadium.

...Medieval peasants had perfect teeth.

...Any person waking from a nightmare will sit bolt upright and pant.

...It is not necessary to say hello or good-bye when beginning or ending phone conversations.

...Even when driving down a perfectly straight road it is necessary to turn the steering wheel vigorously from left to right every few moments.

...All bombs are fitted with electronic timing devices with large red readouts so you know exactly when they're going to go off.

...It is always possible to park directly outside the building you are visiting.

...A detective can only solve a case once he has been suspended from duty.

...It does not matter if you are heavily outnumbered in a fight involving martial arts - your enemies will wait patiently to attack you one by one by dancing around in a threatening manner until you have knocked out their predecessors.

...When a person is knocked unconscious by a blow to the head, they will never suffer a concussion or brain damage.

...No one involved in a car chase, hijacking, explosion, volcanic eruption or alien invasion will ever go into shock.

...Police departments give their officers personality tests to make sure they are deliberately assigned a partner who is their total opposite.

...When they are alone, all foreigners prefer to speak English to each other.

...Any lock can be picked by a credit card or a paper clip in seconds - unless it's the door to a burning building with a child trapped inside.

...Television news bulletins usually contain a story that affects you personally at that precise moment.

Health and Medicine

Broke?

A man goes into the doctor. He says, "Doc, you gotta check my leg. Something's wrong. Just put your ear up to my thigh, you'll hear it!"

The doctor cautiously placed his ear to the man's thigh only to hear, "Gimme 20 bucks, I really need 20 bucks."

"I've never seen or heard anything like this before, how long has this been going on." The doctor asked.

"That's nothing Doc. put your ear to my knee."

The doctor put his ear to the man's knee and heard it say "Man, I really need 10 dollars, just lend me 10 bucks!!"

"Sir, I really don't know what to tell you. I've never seen anything like this." The doctor was dumbfounded.

"Wait Doc, that's not it. There's more, just put your ear up to my ankle," the man urged him.

The doctor did as the man said and was blown away to hear his ankle plead, "Please, I just need 5 dollars. Lend me 5 bucks please if you will."

"I have no idea what to tell you," the doctor said. "There's nothing about it in my books," he said as he frantically searched all his medical reference books. "I can make a well- educated guess though. Based on life and all my previous experience I can tell you that your leg seems to be broke in three places."

Bulging Eyes and Ears

This middle-aged guy wakes up one morning and notices that his eyes are bulging and his ears are protruding. He becomes very concerned. He goes to his doctor and asks doc what is wrong with him. The doctor told him that he has a rare disease that will require him to take this medication for several months to clear up the disease, however the medication will make his hair fall out permanently.

Several months later the guy's eyes are still bulging and his ears are still protruding, more so now that his hair is gone. This time he goes to a different doctor who informs him that he has a liver problems; that they will have to remove part of his liver. The guy has the surgery, only to find out, months later, his eyes are still bulging and his ears are still protruding.

Determined to find out what is wrong with him he goes to another doctor who tells him that the nerves in his hands are pinching the nerve endings in his ears and his eyes and the only way to resolve the problem is to have his hands amputated. Sadly, the guy lets his hands be amputated.

Months later, the man still has the problem. He goes to another specialist who informs him that the cause is a rare blood disease and that the man only has a few months to live!

The guy is hysterical at this point and resolves that if he only has months to live, he is going to live it up. He goes out to buy a brand- new sports car, new furniture and a new wardrobe. However, when he went to order some custom shirts, the tailor told him he took a seventeen-inch neck.

"No, I've always taken a fifteen-inch neck."

"But sir, you have a seventeen-inch neck."

"Listen -- I'm forty-five years old, and for the past thirty years, I've taken a fifteen-inch neck."

"Okay, I'll do it. But do you know what happens when the neck is too small?"

"What?"

"It makes your eyes bulge out and your ears protrude." the tailor replies.

Doctor Shorts

Let Me Tell You About My Doctor. He is very good.
If you tell him you want a second opinion, he will go out and come in again.

Another time he gave a patient 6 months to live. At the end of the 6 months, the patient hadn't paid his bill, so the doctor gave him another 6 months.

While he was talking to me his nurse came in and said, "Doctor, there is a man here who thinks he is invisible." The doctor said, "Tell him I can't see him."

Another time a man came running in the office and yelled, "Doctor, my son just swallowed a roll of film." The doctor calmly replied, "Let's just wait and see what develops."

One patient came in and said, "Doctor, I have a serious memory problem."
The doctor asked, "When did it start?"
The man replied, "When did what start ?"

I remember once I told my doctor I had a ringing in my ears. His advice: "Don't answer it."

My doctor sure has his share of nut cases.
One said to him, "Doctor, I think I'm a bell."
The doctor gave him some pills and said, "Here, take these, and if they don't work, give me a ring."

Another guy told the doctor that he thought he was a deck of cards.

The doctor simply said, "Go sit over there. I'll deal with you later."

When I told my doctor that I broke my leg in two places, he told me to stop going to those places.

But doctors can be so frustrating.
You wait a month and a half for an appointment.

Then he says, "I wish you had come to me sooner."

House Calls

Old Dr. Carver still made house calls. One afternoon he was called to the Tuttle house. Mrs. Tuttle was in terrible pain.

The doctor came out of the bedroom a minute after he'd gone in and asked Mr. Tuttle, "Do you have a hammer?"

A puzzled Mr. Tuttle went to the garage, and returned with a hammer. The doctor thanked him and went back into the bedroom.

A moment later, he came out and asked, "Do you have a chisel?"

Mr. Tuttle complied with the request.

In the next ten minutes, Dr. Carver asked for and received a pair of pliers a screwdriver and a hacksaw.

The last request got to Mr. Tuttle. He asked, "What are you doing to my wife?"

"Not a thing," replied old doc Carver. "I can't get my instrument bag open."

Milk Bath

A lady went into the grocery and asked for fifty gallons of milk.

The clerk, amazed, asked her what she was going to do with that much milk.

"I have a skin problem and the Doctor prescribed a milk bath."
The clerk asked, "Pasteurized?"
She replied, . . . "No just up to my chin."

No Pressure

An older Jewish gentleman was on the operating table awaiting surgery and he insisted that his son, a renowned surgeon, perform the operation. As he was about to get the anesthesia he asked to speak to his son.

"Yes, Dad, what is it?"

"Don't be nervous, son...do your best and just remember, if it doesn't go well, if something happens to me, your mother is going to come and live with you and your wife...."

X-Ray Evaluation

While making rounds, a doctor points out an X-ray to a group of medical students. "As you can see," she says, "the patient limps because his left fibula and tibia are radically arched. Michael, what would you do in a case like this?"

"Well," ponders the student, "I suppose I'd limp too.

Letters

A Dog's Letters to God

Dear God,

How come people love to smell flowers, but seldom, if ever, smell one another? Where are their priorities?

Dear God,

When we get to Heaven, can we sit on your couch? Or is it the same old story?

Dear God,

Excuse me, but why are there cars named after the jaguar, the cougar, the mustang, the colt, the stingray, and the rabbit, but not one named for a dog? How often do you see a cougar riding around? We dogs love a nice ride! I know every breed cannot have its own model, but it would be easy to rename the Chrysler Eagle the Chrysler Beagle!

Dear God,

If a dog barks his head off in the forest and no human hears him, is he still a bad dog?

Dear God,

When my foster mom's friend comes over to our house, he smells like musk! What's he been rolling around in?

Dear God,

Is it true that in Heaven, dining room tables have on-ramps?

Dear God,

More meatballs, less spaghetti, please.

Dear God,

When we get to the Pearly Gates, do we have to shake hands to get in?

Dear God,

We dogs can understand human verbal instructions, hand signals, whistles, horns, clickers, beepers, scent IDs, electromagnetic energy fields, and Frisbee flight paths. What do humans understand?

Dear God,

Are there dogs on other planets, or are we alone? I have been howling at the moon and stars for a long time, but all I ever hear back is the beagle across the street!

Dear God,

Are there mailmen in Heaven? If there are, will I have to apologize?

Dear God,

Is it true that dogs are not allowed in restaurants because we can't make up our minds what NOT to order? Or is it the carpets again?

Dear God,

When my family eats dinner they always bless their food. But, they never bless mine. So, I've been wagging my tail extra fast when they pour fill my bowl. Have you noticed MY blessing?

A Letter to my Son

My Dear Son:

Just a few lines to let you know that I'm still alive. I am writing this letter slowly as I know you can't read fast. You won't know the house when you come home - we've moved.

It was a lot of trouble moving. The most difficult thing was the bed. You see, the man wouldn't let us take it in the taxi. It wouldn't have been so bad if your father hadn't been in it at the time. About your father - he has a lovely new job. He has 500 people under him - he's
cutting grass at the cemetery.

Your sister got herself engaged to that fellow she's been going with. He gave her a beautiful ring with 3 stones missing.

Our neighbors started raising pigs. We got the wind of it this morning. I got my appendix out, and a dishwasher put in. There was a washer machine in the house when we moved in, but it isn't working too well. Last week I put four shirts into it, pulled the chain, and I haven't seen the shirts since.

Your little brother came home from school yesterday crying. All the boys at his school have got new suits. We can't afford to buy him a new suit, but we're going to buy him a new hat and let him stand at the window.

Your sister, Mary, had a baby this morning. I haven't heard yet if it was a boy or a girl - so I don't know if you're an aunt or uncle.

Uncle Dick was drowned last week in a vat of whiskey in Dublin Brewery. Four of his workmates dived in to save him but he fought them off bravely. We cremated his body and it took three days to put out the fire.

Kate is now working in a factory in Birmingham. She's been there for six weeks. I'm sending her some clean underwear as she says she's been in the same shift since she got there.

Your father didn't have too much to drink at Christmas. I put a bottle of castor oil in his pint of scotch and it kept him going until New Year's Day. I went to the doctor on Thursday, your father came too. The doctor put a small glass tube in my mouth and told me to keep it shut for ten minutes. Your father offered to buy it from him.

It only rained twice last week. First for four days and then for three. On Monday it was so windy that one of our chickens laid the same egg four times.

We had a letter from the undertaker. He said if the last installment wasn't paid on your grandmother within seven days - up she comes.

I must close now...the plumber is coming to fix the pipes and there is a shocking smell.

Your loving mother,

P.S. I was going to send you $10.00 but I already sealed the envelope.

Dear Pastor
Dear Pastor,

I know God loves everybody but He never met my sister.
Yours sincerely,
Arnold. Age 8, Nashville.

Dear Pastor,

Please say in your sermon that Peter Peterson has been a good boy all week. I am Peter Peterson. Sincerely,
Pete. Age 9, Phoenix

Dear Pastor,

My father should be a minister. Every day he gives us a sermon about something.

Robert Anderson, age 11

Dear Pastor,
        I'm sorry I can't leave more money in the plate, but my father
didn't give me a raise in my allowance. Could
you have a sermon about a raise in my allowance?
Love,
Patty. Age 10, New Haven

Dear Pastor,
        My mother is very religious. She goes to play
bingo at church every week even if she has a cold.
Yours truly,
Annette. Age 9, Albany

Dear Pastor,
I would like to go to heaven someday because I
know my brother won't be there.
Stephen. Age 8, Chicago

Dear Pastor,
        I think a lot more people would come to your church if you
moved it to Disneyland.
Loreen. Age 9. Tacoma

Dear Pastor,
        I liked your sermon where you said that good
health is more important than money but I still want a raise in my
allowance.
Sincerely,
Eleanor. Age 12, Sarasota

Dear Pastor,
Please pray for all the airline pilots. I am
flying to California tomorrow.
Laurie. Age 10, New York City

Dear Pastor,
I hope to go to heaven some day but later than
sooner.
Love,
Ellen, age 9. Athens

Dear Pastor,
Please say a prayer for our Little League team.
We need God's help or a new pitcher. Thank you. Alexander. Age 10,
Raleigh

Dear Pastor,
My father says I should learn the Ten
Commandments. But I don't think I want to because we have enough
rules already in my house.
Joshua. Age 10, South Pasadena

Dear Pastor,
Who does God pray to? Is there a God for God?
Sincerely,
Christopher. Age 9, Titusville

Dear Pastor,
Are there any devils on earth? I think there
may be one in my class.
Carla. Age 10, Salina

Dear Pastor,
I liked your sermon on Sunday. Especially when
it was finished.

Ralph, Age 11, Akron

Dear Pastor,
    How does God know the good people from the bad
people? Do you tell Him or does He read about it in the newspapers?
Sincerely,
Marie. Age 9, Lewiston

In the Army Now:
Mr. and Mrs. Braithwaite Backus,
Bald Buzzard Ridge, RFD 2
Mountainville, Kentucky

Dear Ma and Pa:
    Am well. Hope you are. Tell Brother Walt and Brother Elmer the
Army beats working for Old Man Minch a mile. Tell them to join up
quick before maybe all the places are filled. I was restless at first
because you got to stay in bed till nearly 6 a.m. (!) but am getting so I
like to sleep late.
    Tell Walt and Elmer all you do before breakfast is smooth your
cot and shine some things -- no hogs to slop, feed to pitch, mash to mix,
wood to split, fire to lay. Practically nothing. You got to shave, but it is
not bad in warm water.
    Breakfast is strong on trimmings like fruit juice, cereal, eggs,
bacon, etc., but kind of weak on chops, potatoes, beef, ham steak, fried
eggplant, pie and regular food. But tell Walt and Elmer you can always
sit between two city boys that live on coffee. Their food plus yours holds
you till noon, when you get fed. It's no wonder these city boys can't
walk much.
    We go on "route marches," which, the Sgt. says, are long walks

to harden us. If he thinks so, it is not my place to tell him different. A "route march" is about as far as to our mailbox at home. Then the city guys all get sore feet and we ride back in trucks.

The country is nice, but awful flat. The Sgt. is like a schoolteacher. He nags some. The Capt. is like the school board. Cols. and Gens. just ride around and frown. They don't bother you none.

This next will kill Walt and Elmer with laughing. I keep getting medals for shooting. I don't know why. The bull's-eye is near as big as a chipmunk and don't move. And it ain't shooting at you, like the Higsett boys at home. All you got to do is lie there all comfortable and hit it. You don't even load your own cartridges. They come in boxes.

Be sure to tell Walt and Elmer to hurry and join before other fellows get onto this setup and come stampeding in.
Your loving son,
Zeb

Letters of Recommendation for Employees

For the chronically absent:
"A man like him is hard to find."
"It seemed his career was just taking off."

For the office drunk:
"I feel his real talent is wasted here."
"We generally found him loaded with work to do."

For an employee with no ambition:
"He could not care less about the number of hours he had to put in."
"You would indeed be fortunate to get this person to work for you."
"He consistently achieves the standards he sets for himself."

For an employee who is so unproductive that the job is better left unfilled:

"I can assure you that no person would be better for the job."

For an employee who is not worth further consideration as a job candidate:

"I would urge you to waste no time in making this candidate an offer of employment."

"All in all, I cannot say enough good things about this candidate or recommend him too highly."

Plow the Potatoes

An old man lived alone in Idaho. He wanted to spade his potato garden, but it was very hard work. His only son, Bubba, who used to help him, was in prison. The old man wrote a letter to his son and described his predicament.

Dear Bubba,

I am feeling pretty bad because it looks like I won't be able to plant my potato garden this year. I'm just getting too old to be digging up a garden plot. If you were here, all my troubles would be over. I know you would dig the plot for me. ....
Love Dad

A few days later he received a letter from his son –

Dear Dad,

For heaven's sake, Dad, don't dig up that garden, that's where I buried the BODIES.

Love Bubba

At 4 am the next morning, FBI agents and local police showed up and dug up the entire area without finding any bodies. They apologized to the old man and left. That same day the old man received another letter from his son.

Dear Dad,
Go ahead and plant the potatoes now. That's the best I could do

under the circumstances. ....

Love Bubba

Life and Work

Bubba

Bubba was bragging to his boss one day, "You know, I know everyone there is to know.   Just name someone, anyone, and I know them."

Tired of his boasting, his boss called his bluff, "OK, Bubba how about Tom Cruise?"

"Sure, yes, Tom and I are old friends, and I can prove it."

So Bubba and his boss fly out to Hollywood and knock on Tom Cruise's door, and sure enough, Tom Cruise, shouts, "Bubba! Great to see you! You and your friend come right in and join me for lunch!"

Although impressed, Bubba's boss is still skeptical. After they leave Cruise's house, he tells Bubba that he thinks Bubba's knowing Cruise was just lucky.

"No, no, just name anyone else," Bubba says.

"President Trump, " his boss quickly retorts.

"Yes," Bubba says, "I know him, let's fly out to Washington."

And off they go. At the White House, Trump spots Bubba on the tour and motions him and his boss over, saying, "Bubba, what a surprise, I was just on my way to a meeting, but you and your friend come on in and let's have a cup of coffee first and catch up."

Well, the boss is very shaken by now, but still not totally convinced. After they leave the White House grounds, he expresses his doubts to Bubba, who again implores him to name anyone else.

"The Pope," his boss replies.

"Sure!" says Bubba. "I've got family in Argentina, and I've known the Pope a long time."

So off they fly to Rome. Bubba and his boss are assembled with the masses in Vatican Square when Bubba says, "This will never work. I can't catch the Pope's eye among all these people. Tell you what, I know all the guards so let me just go upstairs and I'll come out on the balcony with the Pope." And he disappears into the crowd headed toward the Vatican.

Sure enough, half an hour later Bubba emerges with the Pope on the balcony. But by the time Bubba returns, he finds that his boss has had a heart attack and is surrounded by paramedics.

Working his way to his boss' side, Bubba asks him, "What happened?"

His boss looks up and says, "I was doing fine until you and the Pope came out on the balcony and the man next to me said, "Who's that on the balcony with Bubba?"

Good Workout

My grandfather worked in a blacksmith shop when he was a boy, and he used to tell me, when I was a little boy myself, how he had toughened himself up so he could stand the rigors of blacksmithing.

One story was how he had developed his arm and shoulder muscles. He said he would stand outside behind the house and, with a 5 pound potato sack in each hand, extend his arms straight out to his sides and hold them there as long as he could.

After a while he tried 10 pound potato sacks, then 50 pound potato sacks and finally he got to where he could lift a 100 pound potato sack in each hand and hold his arms straight out for more than a full minute!

Next, he started putting potatoes in the sacks.

Run Forrest, Run!

Two gas company servicemen, a senior training supervisor and a young trainee, were out checking meters in a suburban neighborhood. They parked their truck the end of the alley and worked their way to the other end. At the last house, a woman looking out her kitchen window watched the two men as they checked her gas meter.

Finishing the meter check, the senior supervisor challenged his younger coworker to a foot race down the alley back to the truck to prove that an older guy could outrun a younger one.

As they came running up to the truck, they realized the lady from that last house was huffing and puffing right behind them. They stopped and asked her what was wrong.

Gasping for breath, she replied, "When I see two men from the gas company running as hard as you two were, I figured I'd better run too!"

The Equipped Volunteer

After volunteering to fight for his country in WW II, Zimmerman joined his unit and lined up for his uniform. As equipment was issued in strict alphabetical order Zimmerman found himself at the back of the queue. By the time he reached the desk all the uniforms had been issued. There were none left. Zimmerman was issued with a badge that said "soldier" in red letters.

"You didn't want a scratchy old uniform anyway," the quartermaster said. "Join the line for your rifle."

Zimmerman joined the back of the rifle queue. When he reached the front Zimmerman found that all the rifles had been distributed and then, once again, there were none left.

"You don't want to kill people anyway," said the quartermaster. "I'll issue you with a stick and you can shout Bang, Bang! Join the line for your bayonet."

"Thank you," said Zimmerman, and joined the queue for bayonets.

Once again, on reaching the desk Zimmerman was disappointed. The quartermaster issued him with a lollipop stick with the advice that he should shout "Sticky-sticky" when using it.....And so on.

Within weeks Zimmerman found himself on the front lines shouting "Bang-bang" for all he was worth. On his second day the German enemy began a mass advance. One by one Zimmerman's unit were killed or wounded until only Zimmerman himself remained standing. "Bang-bang!" he shouted, and was amazed to see his German foes still falling. Soon they began to overwhelm his trench and Zimmerman began to stab wildly with his lollipop stick. "Sticky-sticky. Sticky-sticky."

Astoundingly it worked. The enemy were dying at his feet. The survivors began to retreat. All, that is, with the exception of one man who was only half way across no-man's land and was still advancing slowly. Zimmerman took careful aim with his stick-rifle and calmly said; "Bang-Bang." The enemy soldier continued his advance. "Bang-bang, bang-bang, bangedy-bang-bang-bang," Zimmerman yelled frantically. Still he came. Before he could reach the trench Zimmerman leapt up and ran at him with the lollipop stick. "Sticky-sticky, he said. And then added "Stab-stab-stab," for good measure.

The enemy soldier refused to die and stared at Zimmerman defiantly. By now Zimmerman had had enough. "Wait a minute, " he said. "When I shouted 'Bang' your comrades died, but not you. When I engaged them in hand-to-hand combat with my lollipop stick they fell over dead, but not you. What gives?" .....

"I'm a tank, " said Herr Zanker.

The Pirates Hook

An able-bodied seaman meets a pirate in a saloon. They start swapping sea stories.

Noting the pirate's peg leg, hook, & eye patch the seaman asks, "So, how did you end up with the peg leg?"

The pirate replies, "We was caught in a monster storm off the cape & a giant wave swept me overboard. Just as they were pullin' me out, a school of sharks swum up & one of 'em chomped me leg clean off."

"Blimey!" said the sailor. "What about the hook?"

"Ahhhh...," mused the pirate, "we were boardin' a trader ship, pistols blastin' & cutlasses swingin' this way & that. In the fracas me hand got hacked off."

"Zounds!" remarked the seaman. "And how came ye by the eye patch?"

"A seagull droppin' fell into me eye," answered the pirate.

"You lost your eye to a seagull dropping?" the sailor asked?

"Aye," said the pirate. "It was me first day with the hook."

War Stories

Down at the veteran's hospital, a trio of old timers ran out of tales of their own heroic exploits and started bragging about their ancestors.

"My great-grandfather, at age 13," one declared proudly, "was a drummer boy at Shiloh."

"Mine," boasted another, "went down with Custer at the Battle of Little Big Horn."

"I'm the only soldier in my family," confessed vet number three, "but if my great-grandfather was living today he'd be the most famous man in the world."

"What's he do?" his friends wanted to know.

"Nothing much. But he would be 165 years old."

Watch Your Language

One reason the Armed Services have trouble operating jointly is that they have very different meanings for the same terms.

The Joint Chiefs once told the Navy to "secure a building," to which they responded by turning off the lights and locking the doors.

The Joint Chiefs then instructed Army personnel to "secure the building," and they occupied the building so no one could enter.

Upon receiving the exact same order, the Marines assaulted the building, captured it, and set up defenses with suppressive fire & amphibious assault vehicles, established reconnaissance and communications channels, and prepared for close hand-to-hand combat if the situation arose.

But the Air Force, on the other hand, acted most swiftly on the command, and took out a three-year lease with an option to buy.

Love, Marriage and Family

A touching story about love and marriage

An elderly man lay dying in his bed. In death's agony, he suddenly smelled the aroma of his favorite chocolate chip cookies wafting up the stairs.

He gathered his remaining strength, and lifted himself from the bed. Leaning against the wall, he slowly made his way out of the bedroom, and with even greater effort forced himself down the stairs, gripping the railing with both hands. With labored breath, he leaned against the door-frame, gazing into the kitchen.

Were it not for death's agony, he would have thought himself already in heaven: there, spread out upon newspapers on the kitchen table were literally hundreds of his favorite chocolate chip cookies.

Was it heaven? Or, was it one final act of heroic love from his devoted wife, seeing to it that he left this world a happy man?

Mustering one great final effort, he threw himself toward the table, landing on his knees in a rumpled posture. His parched lips parted; the wondrous taste of the cookie was already in his mouth; seemingly bringing him back to life.

The aged and withered hand, shakingly made its way to a cookie at the edge of the table, when it was suddenly smacked with a spatula by his wife.

"Stay out of those!" she said, "They're for the funeral."

Baby Name Ideas,   Based on your occupation!
Profession   Name

Profession	Name
Lawyer's daughter	Sue
Thief's son	Rob
Lawyer's son	Will
Doctor 's son	Bill
Meteorologist's daughter	Haley
Steam shovel operator's son	Doug
Hair stylist's son	Bob
Homeopathic doctor's son	Herb
Justice of the peace's daughter	Mary
Sound stage technician's son	Mike
Hot-dog vendor's son	Frank
Gambler's daughter	Bette
Exercise guru's son	Jim
Cattle thief's son	Russell
Gardener's son	Moe
Painter's son	Art
Iron worker's son	Rusty
TV show star's daughter	Emmy
Movie star's son	Oscar
Barber's son	Harry
Housewife's son	Dusty
Minister's daughter	Faith
Day-trader's daughter	Hope
Televangelist's daughter	Charity
IRS agent's daughter	Mony
Geneticist's son	Gene
Espresso vendor's son	Joe
Undertaker's son	Barry
Beautician's son	Curly
Florist's daughter	Rose

Bank Robber

Man robs a bank and takes hostages. He asks the first hostage if he saw him rob the bank.

Hostage answers, "yes."

Robber shoots him. He asks the second hostage if he saw him rob the bank.

Hostage answers "yes."

Robber shoots him. He asks the third hostage if he saw him rob the bank.

Hostage answers, "No, but my wife did."

Communication

While attending a marriage seminar on communication, Jim and his wife listened to the instructor declare: "It is essential that husbands and wives know the things that are important to each other."

He addressed the men: "For instance, gentlemen, can you name your wife's favorite flower?"

Jim leaned over, touched his wife's arm gently and whispered, "Pillsbury All-Purpose, isn't it?"

The rest of the story is not pleasant.

Doilies

As a new bride, Aunt Edna moved into the small home on her husband's ranch near Snowflake. She put a shoe box on a shelf in her closet and asked her husband never to touch it. For 50 years Uncle Jack left the box alone, until Aunt Edna was old and dying. One day when he was putting their affairs in order, he found the box again and thought it might hold something important. Opening it, he found two doilies and $82,500 in cash. He took the box to her and asked about the contents.

"My mother gave me that box the day we married," she

explained. "She told me to make a doily to help ease my frustrations every time I got mad at you."

Uncle Jack was very touched that in 50 years she'd only been mad at him twice.

"What's the $82,500 for?" he asked.

"Oh, well that's is the money I've made selling the Doilies."

Four Seconds or Less

A couple had been debating the purchase of a new auto for weeks. He wanted a new truck. She wanted a fast, little sports-like car so she could zip through traffic around town.

He would probably have settled on any beat- up old truck, but everything she seemed to like was way out of their price range.

"Look!" she said. "I want something that goes from 0 to 200 in 4 seconds or less. "And my birthday is coming up. You could surprise me."

For her birthday, he bought her a brand- new bathroom scale.

Services will be at Downing funeral home on Monday the 12th, due to the condition of the body, this will be a closed casket service.

Hello Honey

There are several men in the locker room of a private club after exercising. Suddenly a cell phone on one of the benches rings. A man picks it up and the following conversation ensues

"Hello?"

"Honey, It's me."

"Sugar!"

"Are you at the club?"

"Yes."

"Great! I'm at the mall 2 blocks from where you are. I saw a beautiful mink coat. It is absolutely gorgeous!! Can I buy it?"

"What's the price?"

"Only $1,500."

"Well, okay, go ahead and get it, if you like it that much."

"Ahhh, and I also stopped by the Mercedes dealership and saw the new models. I saw one I really liked. I spoke with the salesman and he gave me a really good price ... and since we need to exchange the BMW that we bought last year..."

"What price did he quote you?"

"Only $90,000!"

"Okay, but for that price I want it with all the options."

"Great! Before we hang up, something else..."

"What?"

"It might seem like a lot, but I was reconciling your bank account and...well, I stopped by to see the real estate agent this morning and I saw the house we had looked at last year. It's on sale!! Remember? The one with a pool, English garden, acre of park area, beach front property..."

"How much are they asking?"

"Only $1.5million... a magnificent price, and I see that we have that much in the bank to cover..."

"Well, then go ahead and buy it, but just bid $1.4. okay?"

"Okay, sweetie. Thanks! I'll see you later!! I love you!!!"

"Bye. I do too."

The man hangs up, and raises his hand while holding the phone and asks to all those present, "Does anyone know whose phone this is?

Home for the Holidays

An elderly man in Phoenix calls his son Bob in New York and says, "I hate to ruin your day, but your mother and I are divorcing. Forty-five years of misery is enough! I'm sick of her, and I'm sick of talking about this, so call your sister in Boston and tell her," and then hangs up.

The son frantically calls his sister, who goes nuts upon hearing the news.

She calls her father and yells, "You are not getting a divorce!

Bob and I will be there tomorrow. Until then, don't do a single thing, do you hear me?"

The father hangs up the phone, turns to his wife, and says, "It worked! The kids are coming for a visit, and they're paying their own way!"

Honestly!

A police officer pulls over a speeding car. The officer says, "I clocked you at 80 miles per hour, sir."

The driver says, "Gee, officer I had it on cruise control at 60, perhaps your radar gun needs calibrating.

Not looking up from her knitting the wife says: "Now don't be silly dear, you know that this car doesn't have cruise control."

As the officer writes out the ticket, the driver looks over at his wife and growls, "Can't you please keep your mouth shut for once?"

The wife smiles demurely and says, "You should be thankful your radar detector went off when it did."

As the officer makes out the second ticket for the illegal radar detector unit, the man glowers at his wife and says through clenched teeth, "Dang it, woman, can't you keep your mouth shut?"

The officer frowns and says, "And I notice that you're not wearing your seat belt, sir. That's an automatic $75 fine."

The driver says, "Yeah, well, you see officer, I had it on, but took it off when you pulled me over so that I could get my license out of my back pocket.'"

The wife says, "Now, dear, you know very well that you didn't have your seat belt on. You never wear your seat belt when you're driving."

As the police officer is writing out the third ticket the driver turns to his wife and barks, "WHY DON'T YOU PLEASE SHUT UP?"

The officer looks over at the woman and asks, "Does your husband always talk to you this way, Ma'am?"

"Only when he's been drinking."

How You Look at It

A young couple moves into a new neighborhood. The next morning while they are eating breakfast, the young woman sees her neighbor hanging the wash outside.

"That laundry is not very clean," she said. "She doesn't know how to wash correctly. Perhaps she needs better laundry soap."

Her husband looked on, but remained silent. Every time her neighbor would hang her wash to dry, the young woman would make the same comments.

About one month later, the woman was surprised to see a nice clean wash on the line and said to her husband: "Look, she has learned how to wash correctly. I wonder who taught her this?"

The husband said, "I got up early this morning and cleaned our windows."

Marriage Quips

The best way to get most husbands to do something is to suggest that perhaps they're too old to do it.
Ann Bancroft

I think men who have a pierced ear are better prepared for marriage. They've experienced pain and bought jewelry.   Rita Rudner

Keep your eyes wide open before marriage, half shut afterwards. Benjamin Franklin

My wife dresses to kill. She cooks the same way.
Henny Youngman

My wife and I were happy for twenty years. Then we met.
Rodney Dangerfield

A good wife always forgives her husband when she's wrong. Milton Berle

I was married by a judge. I should have asked for a jury. George Burns

What's the difference between a boyfriend and a husband? About 30 pounds.   Cindy Garner

When women are depressed, they either eat or go shopping. Men invade another country. It's a whole different way of thinking. Elaine Boosler

I bought my wife a new car. She called and said, "There was water in the carburetor." I said, "Where's the car?" She said, "In the lake." Henny Youngman

Never go to bed mad. Stay up and fight.   Phyllis Diller

The secret of a happy marriage remains a secret. Henny Youngman

People are always asking couples whose marriages have endured at least a quarter of a century for their secret for success. Actually, it is no secret at all. I am a forgiving woman. Long ago, I forgave my husband for not being Paul Newman.   Erma Bombeck

"Honest criticism is hard to take, particularly from a relative, a friend, an acquaintance, or a stranger." Franklin P. Jones

"How far you go in life is determined by how tender you are with the young, compassionate with the aged, sympathetic with those striving, and tolerant with the weak and strong, because some day in life you will have been all of them."

Remember Great-Grandpa Joe?

The family all knew the story of Grandpa's ne'er-do-well father, the one who was hung as a horse thief after escaping from prison, where he wound up after robbing a bank and a train. They couldn't leave him out of the family history, but they could and did put some spin on the story.

The "official" family version of his demise went something like this:

"Joseph James was a famous cowboy in the Montana Territory. He spent a period of time on the fast track with Wells Fargo. His business empire grew to include acquisition of valuable equestrian assets. He devoted several years of his life to service at a government facility, finally taking leave to resume his dealings with other equestrian entrepreneurs. Joe James passed away during an important civic function held in his honor when the platform upon which he was standing collapsed."

Secret of Success

At Saint Mary's Catholic Church they have a weekly husband's marriage seminar. At a session, last week, the Priest asked Luigi, who was approaching his 50th wedding anniversary, to take a few, minutes and share some insight into how he had managed to stay married to the same woman all these years.

Luigi replied to the assembled husbands, "Well, I've a-tried to treat-a her nice, spend the money on her, but best is that I took-a her to Italy for the 20th anniversary!"

The Priest responded, "Luigi, you are an amazing inspiration to all the husbands here! Please tell us what you are planning for your wife for your 50th anniversary."

Luigi proudly replied, "I'm a-gonna go to get her."

Sweet Revenge

The wedding day was fast approaching. Everything was ready, and nothing could dampen Jennifer's excitement, not even her parents' nasty divorce. Her mother Sheila finally found the PERFECT dress to wear and would be the best-dressed mother of the bride EVER!

A week later, Jennifer was horrified to learn her new young stepmother, Barbie, had purchased the same dress. She asked Barbie to exchange the dress, but Barbie refused, "Absolutely not! I'm going to wear this dress. I'll look like a million bucks in it!"

Jennifer told her mother, who graciously replied, "Never mind, dear. I'll get another dress, after all it's YOUR special day, not ours."

Two weeks later, another dress was finally found. When they stopped for lunch, Jennifer asked her mother, "What are you going to do with the first dress? Maybe you should return it. You don't have any place to wear it."

Sheila grinned and replied, "Of course, I do, dear. I'm wearing it to the rehearsal dinner."

Sweeter Revenge

She spent the first day packing her belongings into boxes, crates and suitcases. On the second day, she had the movers come and collect her things. On the third day, she sat down for the last time at their beautiful dining room table by candlelight, put on some soft background music, and feasted on a pound of shrimp, a jar of caviar, and a bottle of Chardonnay. When she had finished, she went into each and every room and deposited a few half-eaten shrimp shells, dipped in caviar, into the hollow of the curtain rods. She then cleaned up the kitchen and left.

When the husband returned with his new girlfriend, all was bliss for the first few days. Then slowly, the house began to smell. They tried everything; cleaning and mopping and airing the place out. Vents were checked for dead rodents, and carpets were steam cleaned. Air fresheners were hung everywhere. Exterminators were brought in to set off gas canisters, during which they had to move out for a few days, and in the end they even paid to replace the expensive wool carpeting. Nothing worked. People stopped coming over to visit... Repairmen refused to work in the house...The maid quit...Finally, they could not take the stench any longer and decided to move. A month later, even though they had cut their price in half, they could not find a buyer for their stinky house. Word got out, and eventually, even the local Realtors refused to return their calls. Finally, they had to borrow a huge sum of money from the bank to purchase a new place.

The ex-wife called the man, and asked how things were going. He told her the saga of the rotting house. She listened politely, and said that she missed her old home terribly, and would be willing to reduce her divorce settlement in exchange for getting the house back...

Knowing his ex-wife had no idea how bad the smell was, he agreed on price that was about 1/10th of what the house had been worth...But only if she were to sign the papers that very day. She agreed, and within the hour, his lawyers delivered the paperwork.

A week later, the man and his new girlfriend stood smirking as they watched the moving company pack everything to take to their new home......including the curtain rods.

That Mad?

Late one Saturday evening, a woman was awakened by the ringing of her phone. In a sleepy grumpy voice she said hello. The party on the other end of the line paused for a moment before rushing breathlessly into a lengthy speech.

"Mom, this is Susan and I'm sorry I woke you up, but I had to call because I'm going to be a little late getting home. See, Dad's car has a flat but it's not my fault. Honest! I don't
know what happened. The tire just went flat while we were inside the

concert hall. Please don't be mad, okay?"

Since the woman didn't have any daughters, she knew the person had mis-dialed. "I'm sorry dear, "she replied, "but you've reached the wrong number. I don't have a daughter named Susan."

A pause. Then, "Boy, Mom," came the young woman's voice, "I didn't think you'd be this mad."

The Perfect Gift

There was this little old lady who was nearly blind and she had three sons who wanted to prove which one was the best son to her.

So son # 1 bought her a 15 room mansion thinking this would surely be the best any of them could offer her.

Son # 2 bought her a beautiful Mercedes with a chauffeur included thinking her would surely win her approval.

Son # 3 had to do something even better than these so he bought her a trained parrot that had been training for 15 years to memorize the entire Bible. You could ask of him any verse in the Bible and the parrot could quote it word for word. What a gift that would be.

Well, the old lady went to the first son and said, "Son, the house is just gorgeous but it's really much too big for me. I only live in one room, and it's much too large for me to clean and take care of. I really don't need the house, but thank you anyway."

Then she confronted her second son with "Son, the car is beautiful, it has everything you could ever want on it, but I don't drive and I really don't like that driver, so please return the car."

Next, she went to son number three and said, "Son I just want to thank you for that most thoughtful gift. That chicken was delicious."

The Woman and 3 Wishes

A woman was out golfing one day when she hit her ball into the woods. She went into the woods to look for it and found a frog in a trap.

The frog said to her, "If you release me from this trap, I will grant you 3 wishes."

The woman freed the frog and the frog said, "Thank you, but I failed to mention that there was a condition to your wishes-that whatever you wish for, your husband will get 10 times more or better!"

The woman said, "That would be okay," and for her first wish, she wanted to be the most beautiful woman in the world.

The frog warned her, "You do realize that this wish will also make your husband the most handsome man in the world, an Adonis, that women will flock to."

The woman replied, "That will be okay because I will be the most beautiful woman and he will only have eyes for me." So, KAZAM - she's the most beautiful woman in the world!

For her second wish, she wanted to be the richest woman in the world.

The frog said, "That will make your husband the richest man in the world and he will be ten times richer than you."

The woman said, "That will be okay because what is mine is his and what is his is mine."

So, KAZAM she's the richest woman in the world!

The frog then inquired about her third wish, and she answered, "I'd like a mild heart attack."

Moral of the story: Women are clever. Don't mess with them.

Three Strikes

The old bachelor farmer decided to finally tie the knot and get married. After the ceremony, they were loading the buckboard to drive home and their old mule kicked a couple of times knocking the wagon. The old farmer said, "That's one."

As they were driving down the lane, a rabbit jumped out in front of the mule and he skirmished a little as the old farmer said, "That's two."

Continuing toward home, the old mule saw some refreshing grass and decided to stop and graze. The old farmer said, "That's three," and got out and shot the mule dead where it stood.

The wife, not quiet knowing what to make of the situation, stood up on the buckboard and said, "Now, Hiram. That's no way to treat a defenseless mule."

The old farmer looked up from the mule, looked at his wife, and said, "That's one."

Mothers

A MOTHER'S SECRETS

A mother is driving her little girl to her friend's house for a play date. "Mommy," the little girl asks, "how old are you?"

"Honey, you are not supposed to ask a lady her age," the mother replied. "It's not polite."

"OK," the little girl says. "'How much do you weigh?"

"Now really," the mother says, "those are personal questions and are really none of your business."

Undaunted, the little girl asks, "Why did you and Daddy get a divorce?"

"That's enough questions, young lady! Honestly!" The exasperated mother walks away as the two friends begin to play.

"My Mom won't tell me anything about her," the little girl says to her friend.

"Well," says the friend, "all you need to do is look at her driver's license. It's like a report card. It has everything on it."

Later that night the little girl says to her mother, "I know how old you are. You are 32."

The mother is surprised and asks, "How did you find that out?"

"I also know that you weigh 130 pounds."

The mother is past surprised and shocked now. "How in Heaven's name did you find that out?"

"And," the little girl says triumphantly, "I know why you and daddy got a divorce."

"Oh really?" the mother asks. "Why?"

"Because you got an F in sex."

Exasperated Mother

An exasperated mother, whose son was always getting into mischief, finally asked him, "How do you expect to get into heaven?"

The boy thought it over and said, "Well, I'll just run in and out and in and out and keep slamming the door until St. Peter says, 'For heaven's sake, Jimmy, come in or stay out.'"

From the library

A little boy walked up to the librarian to check out a book entitled "COMPREHENSIVE GUIDE FOR MOTHERS."

When the librarian asked him if it was for his mother, he answered "no."

"Then why are you checking it out?"

"Because," said the boy, beaming from ear to ear, ... "I just started collecting moths last month!"

Going To Bed

Mom and Dad were watching TV when Mom said, "I'm tired, and it's getting late. I think I'll go to bed."

She went to the kitchen to make sandwiches for the next day's lunches, rinsed out the popcorn bowls, took meat out of the freezer for supper the following evening, checked the cereal box levels, filled the sugar container, put spoons and bowls on the table and started the coffee pot for brewing the next morning.

She then put some wet clothes into the dryer, put a load of clothes into the wash, ironed a shirt and secured a loose button. She picked up the newspapers strewn on the floor, picked up the game pieces left on the table and put the telephone book back into the drawer. She watered the plants, emptied a wastebasket and hung up a towel to dry.

She yawned and stretched and headed for the bedroom. She stopped by the desk and wrote a note to the teacher, counted out some cash for the field trip, and pulled a textbook out from hiding under the chair. She signed a birthday card for a friend, addressed and stamped the envelope and wrote a quick note for the grocery store. She put both near her purse.

Mom then washed her face, put on moisturizer, brushed and flossed her teeth and trimmed her nails.

Hubby called, "I thought you were going to bed."

"I'm on my way," she said.

She put some water into the dog's dish and put the cat outside, then made sure the doors were locked. She looked in on each of the kids and turned out a bedside lamp, hung up a shirt, threw some dirty socks in the hamper, and had a brief conversation with the one up still doing homework.

In the bedroom, she set the alarm, laid out clothing for the next day, straightened up the shoe rack. She added three things to her list of things to do for tomorrow.

About that time, hubby turned off the TV and announced to no one in particular "I'm going to bed." And, he did.

HOW TO BAKE A CAKE

(Dedicated to all mothers everywhere)

Preheat oven, get out utensils and ingredients.
Remove blocks and toy cars from table.
Grease pan, crack nuts.
Measure two cups flour.
Remove baby's hands from flour, wash flour off baby.
Remeasure flour.
 Put flour, baking powder, salt in sifter.
Get dustpan and brush up pieces of bowl baby knocked on floor.

Get another bowl.
Answer doorbell.
Return to kitchen.
Remove baby's hands from bowl.
Wash baby.
Answer phone.
Return.
Remove 1/4 inch salt from greased pan.
Look for baby.
Grease another pan.
Answer telephone.
Return to kitchen and find baby.
Remove baby's hands from bowl.
Take up greased pan, find layer of nutshells in it.
Head for baby, who flees, knocking bowl off table.
Wash kitchen floor, table, wall, dishes.
Call baker.
Lie down.

Mothers Said:
PAUL REVERE'S MOTHER: "I don't care where you think you have to go, young man. Midnight is past your curfew!"

MARY, MARY, QUITE CONTRARY'S MOTHER: "I don't mind you having a garden, Mary, but does it have to be growing under your bed?"

MONA LISA'S MOTHER: "After all that money your father and I spent on braces, Mona, that's the biggest smile you can give us?"

HUMPTY DUMPTY'S MOTHER: "Humpty, if I've told you once, I've told you a hundred times not to sit on that wall. But would you listen to me? Noooo!"

COLUMBUS' MOTHER: "I don't care what you've discovered, Christopher. You still could have written!"

BABE RUTH'S MOTHER: "Babe, how many times have I told you--quit playing ball in the house! That's the third broken window this week!"

MICHELANGELO'S MOTHER: "Mike, can't you paint on walls like other children? Do you have any idea how hard it is to get that stuff off the ceiling?"

NAPOLEON'S MOTHER: "All right, Napoleon. If you aren't hiding your report card inside your jacket, then take your hand out of there and prove it!"

CUSTER'S MOTHER: "Now, George, remember what I told you--don't go biting off more than you can chew!"

ABRAHAM LINCOLN'S MOTHER: "Again with the stovepipe hat, Abe? Can't you just wear a baseball cap like the other kids?"

BARNEY'S MOTHER: "I realize strained plums are your favorite, Barney, but you're starting to look a little purple."

MARY'S MOTHER: "I'm not upset that your lamb followed you to school, Mary, but I would like to know how he got a better grade than you."

BATMAN'S MOTHER: "It's a nice car, Bruce, but do you realize how much the insurance is going to be?"

GOLDILOCKS' MOTHER: "I've got a bill here for a busted chair from the Bear family. You know anything about this, Goldie?"

LITTLE MISS MUFFET'S MOTHER: "Well, all I've got to say is if you don't get off your tuffet and start cleaning your room, there'll be a lot more spiders around here!"

ALBERT EINSTEIN'S MOTHER: "But, Albert, it's your senior picture. Can't you do something about your hair? Styling gel, mousse, something...?"

GEORGE WASHINGTON'S MOTHER: "The next time I catch you throwing money across the Potomac, you can kiss your allowance good-bye!"

JONAH'S MOTHER: "That's a nice story, but now tell me where you've really been for the last three days."

SUPERMAN'S MOTHER: "Clark, your father and I have discussed it, and we've decided you can have your own telephone line. Now will you quit spending so much time in all those phone booths?"

THOMAS EDISON'S MOTHER: "Of course I'm proud that you invented the electric light bulb, Thomas. Now turn off that light and get to bed!"

Mother's Standards

Congratulating a friend after her son and daughter got married within a month of each other, a woman asked, "What kind of boy did your daughter marry?"

"Oh, he's wonderful," gushed the mother. "He lets her sleep late, wants her to go to the beauty parlor regularly, and insists on taking her out to dinner every night."

"That's sounds lovely," said the woman. "What about your son?"

"I'm not so happy about that," the mother sighed. "His wife sleeps late, spends all her time in the beauty parlor, and makes them eat take-out meals!"

The Secret

A mother was showing her son how to zip up his coat. "The

secret," she said, "is to get the left part of the zipper to fit in the other side before you try to zip it up."

The boy looked at her quizzically, "Why does it have to be a secret?"

Definition of a sweater: Something a child wears when his mother is cold.

The Big M

A teacher gave her class of second graders a lesson on the magnet and what it does. The next day in a written test, she included this question:

"My full name has six letters. The first one is M. I am strong and attractive. I pick up things. What am I?"

When the test papers were turned in, the teacher was astonished to find that almost 50 percent of the students answered the question with the word "Mother."

What Mothers Do

One afternoon a man came home from work to find total mayhem in his house. His three children were outside, still in their pajamas, playing in the mud, with empty food boxes and wrappers strewn all around the front yard.
The door of his wife's car was open, as was the front door to the house.

Proceeding into the entry, he found an even bigger mess. A lamp had been knocked over, and the throw rug was wadded against one wall. In the front room the TV was loudly blaring a cartoon channel, and the family room was
strewn with toys and various items of clothing. In the kitchen, dishes

filled the sink, breakfast food was spilled on the counter, dog food was spilled on the floor, a broken glass lay under the table, and a small pile of sand was spread by the back door.

He quickly headed up the stairs, stepping over toys and more piles of clothes, looking for his wife. He was worried she may be ill, or that something serious had happened. He found her lounging in the bedroom, still
curled in the bed in her pajamas, reading a novel. She looked up at him, smiled, and asked how his day went.

He looked at her bewildered and asked, "What happened here today?"

She again smiled and answered, "You know every day when you come home from work and ask me what in the world I did today?"

"Yes" was his incredulous reply.

She answered, "Well, today I didn't do it."

Music

Bad Tempo

The band leader had a drummer who dragged(duh). After remonstrating with him without success the band leader had to fire him. The drummer was so distraught that he went down to the railway station and threw himself behind a train.

Drummer Needed

Clyde, a nightclub owner hired a pianist and a drummer to entertain the customers. After several performances, he discovered that the drummer had walked away with some of his valuables.

Clyde notified the police, who arrested the thief. Desperate for another drummer, he called a friend who knew some musicians.

"What happened to the drummer you had?" he asked.

"I had him arrested," Clyde replied.

His friend hesitated, then asked, "How badly did he play?"

Handle the Sticks?

A musical director was having a lot of trouble with one drummer. He talked and talked and talked with the drummer, but his performance simply didn't improve.

Finally, before the whole orchestra, he said, "When a musician just can't handle his instrument and doesn't improve when given help, they take away the instrument, and give him two sticks, and make him a drummer."

A stage whisper was heard from the percussion section: "And if he can't handle even that, they take away one of his sticks and make him a conductor."

"The singing of God's praise is the part of worship most closely related to heaven; but its performance among us is the worst on earth."-Issac Watts

"Guys, it doesn't matter how ugly you are, if you can sing, women will love you!"   −Terry Bradshaw

"The principle difference between rock n'' roll and classical music is that your average piece of classical music has about a dozen melodies and no words, whereas your average rock ''n roll song has one melody and about a dozen words." Dave Barry

"Music is the only language in which you cannot say a mean or sarcastic thing." –John Erskine

"Hope is the ability to hear the music of the future. Faith is having the courage to dance to it today."

"A man who wants to lead the orchestra must turn his back on the crowd." - James Crook

Music Shorts

How can you tell the trombone player's kid on the playground? He can't swing and doesn't know how to use the slide.

How many clarinet players does it take to change a lightbulb? Only one, but they'll go through the whole box till they find one they like.

"Welcome to heaven, here's your harp and your tuning key." "Welcome to hell, here's your harp."

General Custer and his aide were in the fort. The aide said, "General, I don't like the sound of those drums."
From over the hill you hear a voice yell, "He's not our regular drummer."

What's the difference between a Tenor sax player and a macaw? One is loud, obnoxious and noisy, and the other is a bird.

What kind of calendar does a trombonist use for his gigs? "Year-at-a-glance"

What's the difference between a lawnmower and a tenor sax? Lawnmowers sound better in small ensembles.

What's the range of the French horn? 30 feet if you get a good grip.

What's the difference between a baritone sax and a vacuum cleaner? The vibrato.

What do pirates and trumpet players have in common? They are both murder on the high C's.

Two tuba players are walking past a bar...Well, it could happen!

What do all great conductors have in common? They're all dead.

Did you hear about the guitar player who was in tune? Neither did I.

What do you throw a drowning guitar player? His Amp.

What's the difference between a cello and a coffin? A coffin has the corpse inside.

What's the difference between a soprano and a piranha?

Lipstick.

How many female singers does it take to sing "Crazy"? Apparently, all of them.

How do you put a twinkle in a female singer's eye? Shine a light in her right ear.

How can you tell when a soprano is at the front door? She can't find the key and doesn't know when to come in.

How do you get two guitar players to play in counterpoint? Have them read off the same part.

How many alto sax players does it take to change a light bulb? Five. One to handle the bulb and four to contemplate how Phil Woods would have done it.

What do you call a beautiful woman on a trombonist's arm? A tattoo.

What do you call a drummer in a three-piece suit? "The Defendant"

What's the similarity between a drummer and a philosopher? They both perceive time as an abstract concept.

Why do some people have an instant aversion to banjo players?
It saves time in the long run.

What's the difference between a guitar player and a large pizza?
A large pizza can feed a family of four.

What's the difference between a jet airplane and a drummer?
About three decibels.

What's the latest crime wave in New York City?
Drive-by trombone solos.

What's the definition of a minor second interval?
Two Soprano Sax players reading off the same part.

What is another term for trombone?
A wind driven, manually operated, pitch approximator.

How do you get an oboist to play A flat?
Take the batteries out of his electronic tuner.

What is the dynamic range of a bass trombone?
On or off.

What's the difference between a SCUD missile and a bad oboist? A bad oboist can kill you.

Why do clarinetists leave their cases on the dashboard? So they can park in the handicapped zones.

What's the difference between a girl singer and a pit bull? Lipstick.

Why do people play trombone?
Because they can't move their fingers and read music at the same time.

What do you call a guitar player that only knows two chords? A music critic.

How do you keep your violin from being stolen?
Put it in a viola case.

What will you never say about a banjo player?
That's the banjo player's Porsche.

What do a viola and a lawsuit have in common?
Everyone is relieved when the case is closed.

Why are harps like elderly parents?
Both are unforgiving and hard to get into and out of cars.

How many trumpet players does it take to pave a driveway?
Seven- if you lay them out correctly.

What's the difference between an oboe and a bassoon? You can hit a baseball further with a bassoon.

How are a banjo player and a blind javelin thrower alike? Both command immediate attention and alarm, and force everyone to move out of range.

What's the best recording of the Walton Violin Concerto?
"Music Minus One"

What's the difference between a Wagnerian soprano and a baby elephant? Eleven pounds.

What's the difference between alto clef and Greek?
Some conductors actually read Greek.

Glissando A technique adopted by string players for difficult runs.

Relative minor A guitarist's girlfriend.

Subito piano- Indicates an opportunity for some obscure orchestra player to become a soloist.

Musica ficta - When you lose your place and have to bluff until you find it again.

Vibrato- Used by singers to hide the fact that they are on the wrong pitch.

What's the difference between a puppy and a singer-songwriter? Eventually the puppy stops whining.

How did the tuba player kill himself? He walked off a clef.

How do musicians pay their debts?
With quarter notes.

Why did the percussionist leave?
He was drummed out of the orchestra.

Why did the opera house fire their male singer?
He was always singing tenor eleven notes off.

Why aren't fish allowed to play in an orchestra?
Because you can tune a piano but you can't tuna fish.

Why did the conductor tell the trumpeter to stop talking? He was always trying to blow his own horn.

What do you call a conductor who is always giving his orchestra grief? A treble maker.

What does a musician use to sign his checks?
A time signature.

Why was the clarinetist always cutting himself?
His music was always too sharp.

What are the three most difficult years in a bass players life?
Second grade.

What do you say to a guitarist in a three- piece suit?
Will the defendant please rise.

How does a guitar player show he's planning for the future? He buys two cases of beer instead of one.

Musical Spat

A tour manager comes across the guitarist and bass player fighting at the side of the stage and pulls them apart asking what the problem was.

"That dummy de-tuned one of the strings on my bass", says the bass player, "And we're on stage in five minutes."

"So what's the problem?", asks the tour manager.

"He won't tell me which string it was he de-tuned", said the Bassist.

Musical Terms

A tempo de cafe -- Ah, coffee time!

Acciaccatura/appoggiatura -- insects

Aleatoric Music: Music composed by the random selection of pitches and rhythms. Frequently found in the performance of the choir anthem.

Allegro -- It's a little car

Antiphonal: Leaving your answering machine on all of the time.
Basso Continuo: When the conductor can't get the jerks to stop singing.

Cantus Firmus: A singer in good physical condition (as opposed to the "cantus flabbioso").

Chords -- things organists play with one finger

Colla Voce -- this shirt is so tight I can't sing

Concerto Grosso: An accordion concert.

Con Moto -- yeah baby, I have a car

Contralto: An alto who has been convicted of a felony.

Discords -- things that organists play with two fingers

Dominant: In a choral relationship, usually the soprano.

Etude: What comes right before the Beatitudes.

f -- forte -- the neighbors are out

ff -- fortissimo -- forget the neighbors

Flats -- English apartments

Fugue -- clever stuff

Glissando: What directly precedes the highest note of the soprano part.

Grand Pause: When the conductor loses his place.

Improvisation -- what you do when the music falls down

Interval -- time to meet the other players at the club

Key Signatures -- silly things put in music to frighten you (ignore and they will go away —— along with your audience)

Leitmotif: Like a regular motif, but less filling.

Lento -- the days leading up to Easter

Melody -- an ancient now-extinct art in song writing

Metronome -- short, urban musician who can fit into a Honda Civic

Music -- happiness

Obbligato -- being forced to practice

p -- piano --the neighbors have complained

pp -- pianissimo -- the neighbors and the police are at the door

Perfect Interval -- when the dinner is on the house

Perfect Pitch: Throwing an accordion into a dumpster w/out hitting the sides.

Prelude -- warm-up before the clever stuff

Professional -- anyone who can't hold down a steady job

Piu Animato -- clean out the cat's little box or it goes

Quaver -- the feeling brought on when you haven't practiced

Riff: What happens when someone takes your choir robe.

Rit/Rall -- coming to the part you haven't practiced

Score: Basses 8, Tenors 0.

Smorzando: The "All-you-can-eat" buffet at Luciano's

Subdominate -- "I can't play unless I've asked my wife."

Syncopation --condition brought on by an overdose of jazz

Theme: We HATE this anthem.

Theme & Variations: We HATE this anthem, the composer, & all his family.

Tonic: A smooth liquid generally enjoyed over ice after choir rehearsal.

Virtuoso -- a person who can work wonders with easy-play music

Say what?
A young child says to his mother, "Mom, when I grow-up I think I'd like to be a musician."
She replies, "Well honey, you know you can't do both."

Trombone Danger
Applying the same logic that brought us "Guns don't kill people, people do," we conclude: Trombones don't play out of tune, trombone players do. Come to think of it, there are other similarities as well. In the wrong hands, a trombone can be a dangerous weapon.
Each year thousands are people are killed, maimed or annoyed by trombones. Trombones should be stored out of reach of children.
There is currently legislation pending in Congress to restrict the sale of trombones and equip them with child-safety devices. The powerful trombone lobby is, of course, opposed to this. There have been various proposals
for requiring a so called "trigger lock."

Efforts to enact a mandatory 10 day waiting period to purchase a trombone have been heretofore been thwarted. This would allow a period of time for
law enforcement to cross check the purchaser's name against a national list of registered trombone offenders.

Law enforcement officials are particularly alarmed over the increase in crimes involving use of the "sawed-off" trombone or "sackbut."

One response is the increased sentencing for those using a trombone while committing a crime (use a trombone - go to jail). This has been especially effective when used in conjunction with the new "Three sharps, you're out" laws passed in many states.

The automatic and semi-automatic models are much more dangerous than the traditional single note trombone. The awesome destructive power of the
double trigger bass trombone could never have been imagined by the founding fathers when they granted us the right to keep and arm bears.

Remember: When trombones are outlawed, only outlaws will play "I'm Gettin' Sentimental Over You".

Trombone Solo

After the last child moves out of the house, Mom and Dad announce that they're getting a divorce. The kids are totally distraught and pay for a session with the world's most famous marriage counselor as a last effort at keeping their parents together. The counselor works for hours, tries all of his methods, but the couple still won't even talk to each other.

Finally, he goes over to a closet, brings out a beautiful trombone and begins to play. After a minute, the couple starts talking. The therapist keeps on soloing on the trombone and the couple discover that they're not actually that far apart and decide to give their marriage another try.

The kids are amazed and ask the doctor how he managed to do

it.

He replies, "Well, I've never yet seen a couple that wouldn't talk through a trombone solo."

Tuba Lessons

A father decided to let his son take tuba lessons. The boy had his first lesson right after school. When he got home his father asked him what he'd learned.

"I learned to play Bb" was the response.

"Good," said the father, "that's a good start."

The next week when he got home the father asked the same question.

"I learned to play F," said the son.

Again, the father was pleased.

The third week the son was late. Supper came and went and he was nowhere to be seen. Finally, he comes walking in at 2 A.M.

"Where have you been?" asked the father.

Said the son, "I had a gig".

Watch This!

Paolo Esperanza, bass-trombonist with the Simphonica Mayor de Uruguay, in a misplaced moment of inspiration decided to make his own contribution to the cannon shots fired as part of the orchestra's performance of Tchaikovsky's 1812 Overture at an outdoor children's concert. In complete seriousness he placed a large, ignited firecracker, which was equivalent in strength to a quarter stick of dynamite, into his aluminum straight mute and then stuck the mute into the bell of his quite new Yamaha in-line bass trombone.

Later, from his hospital bed he explained to a reporter through bandages on his mouth, "I thought that the bell of my trombone would shield me from the explosion and instead, would focus the energy of the blast outwards and away from me, propelling the mute high above the orchestra, like a rocket."

However, Paolo was not up on his propulsion physics nor qualified to use high-powered artillery and in his haste to get the horn up before the firecracker went off, he failed to raise the bell of the horn high enough so as to give the mute enough arc to clear the orchestra.

What actually happened should serve as a lesson to us all during those delirious moments of divine inspiration. First, because he failed to sufficiently elevate the bell of his horn, the blast propelled the mute between rows of players in the woodwind and viola sections of the orchestra, missing the players and straight into the stomach of the conductor, driving him off the podium and directly into the front row of the audience.

Fortunately, the audience were sitting in folding chairs and thus they were protected from serious injury, for the chairs collapsed under them passing the energy of the impact of the flying conductor backwards into row of people sitting behind them, who in turn were driven back into the people in the row behind and so on, like a row of dominos. The sound of collapsing wooden chairs and grunts of people falling on their behinds increased logarithmically, adding to the overall sound of brass cannons and brass playing as constitutes the closing measures of the Overture.

Meanwhile, all of this unplanned choreography notwithstanding, back onstage Paolo's Waterloo was still unfolding. According to Paolo, "Just as the I heard the sound of the blast, time seemed to stand still. Everything moved in slow motion. Just before I felt searing pain to my mouth, I could swear I heard a voice with a Austrian accent say "Fur every akshon zer iz un eekvul un opposeet reakshon!"

Well, this should come as no surprise, for Paolo had set himself up for a textbook demonstration of this fundamental law of physics. Having failed to plug the lead pipe of his trombone, he allowed the energy of the blast to send a super-heated jet of gas backwards through the mouth pipe of the trombone which exited the mouthpiece burning his lips and face.

The pyrotechnic ballet wasn't over yet. The force of the blast was so great it split the bell of his shiny Yamaha right down the middle, turning it inside out while at the same time propelling Paolo backwards off the riser. And for the grand finale, as Paolo fell backwards he lost his grip on the slide of the trombone allowing the pressure of the hot gases coursing through the horn to propel the trombone's slide like a double golden spear into the head of the 3rd clarinetist, knocking him unconscious.

The moral of the story? Beware the next time you hear someone in the trombone section yell out "Hey, everyone, watch this!"

Political

Donkey Raffle

Young Chuck, moved to Texas and bought a Donkey from a farmer for $100.00. The farmer agreed to deliver the Donkey the next day.

The next day he drove up and said, "Sorry son, but I have some bad news, the donkey died."

Chuck replied, "Well, then just give me my money back."

The farmer said, "Can't do that. I went and spent it already."

Chuck said, "Ok, then, just bring me the dead donkey."

The farmer asked, "What ya gonna do with him?"

Chuck said, "I'm going to raffle him off."

The farmer said, "You can't raffle off a dead donkey!"

Chuck said, "Sure I can Watch me.. I just won't tell anybody he's dead."

A month later, the farmer met up with Chuck and asked, "What happened with that dead donkey?"

Chuck said, "I raffled him off. I sold 500 tickets at two dollars a piece and made a profit of $898.00."

The farmer said, "Didn't anyone complain?"

Chuck said, "Just the guy who won. So I gave him his two dollars back."

Chuck now works for the government.

"The reason there are two senators for each state is so that one can be the designated driver." --Jay Leno

"History is a selective interpretation of events designed to justify those currently in power. Memory is the same thing on an individual scale."

The Haircut

One day a florist went to a barber for a haircut. After the cut, he asked about his bill, and the barber replied, 'I cannot accept money from you, I'm doing community service this week.' The florist was pleased and left the
shop.

When the barber went to open his shop the next morning, there was a 'thank you' card and a dozen roses waiting for him at his door.

Later, a cop comes in for a haircut, and when he tries to pay his bill, the barber again replied, 'I cannot accept money from you , I'm doing community service this week.' The cop was happy and left the shop.

The next morning when the barber went to open up, there was a 'thank you' card and a dozen donuts waiting for him at his door.

Then a Congressman came in for a haircut, and when he went to pay his bill, the barber again replied, 'I cannot accept money from you. I'm doing community service this week.' The Congressman was very happy and left the shop.

The next morning, when the barber went to open up, there were a dozen Congressmen lined up waiting for a free haircut.

The Indian and the Buffalo

An Indian walks into a cafe with a shotgun in one hand pulling a male buffalo with the other. He says to the waiter: "Want coffee."

The waiter says, "Sure, Chief, Coming right up." He gets the Indian a tall mug of coffee. The Indian drinks the coffee down in one gulp, turns and blasts the buffalo with the shotgun, causing parts of the animal to splatter everywhere and then he just walks out.

The next morning the Indian returns. He has his shotgun in one hand, pulling another male buffalo with the other. He walks up to the counter and says to the waiter, "Want coffee."

The waiter says "Whoa, Tonto! We're still cleaning up your mess from yesterday. What was all that about, anyway?"

The Indian smiles and proudly says,. "Training for position in United States Congress: Come in, drink coffee, shoot the bull, leave mess for others to clean up, disappear for rest of day.

Yuppie Congressman

A cowboy was overseeing his herd in a remote mountainous pasture in California when suddenly a brand-new BMW advanced toward him out of a cloud of dust. The driver, a young man in a Brioni® suit, Gucci® shoes , RayBan® sunglasses and YSL® tie, leaned out the window and asked the cowboy, "If I tell you exactly how many cows and calves you have in your herd, will you give me a calf?"

The cowboy looks at the man, then looks at his peacefully grazing herd and calmly answers, "Sure, Why not?"

The man parks his car, whips out his notebook computer, connects it to his iphone, and surfs to a NASA page on the Internet, where he calls up a GPS satellite to get an exact fix on his location which he then feeds to another NASA satellite that scans the area in an ultra-high-resolution photo. The young man then opens the digital photo in Adobe Photoshop® and exports it to an image processing facility in Hamburg, Germany. Within seconds, he receives an email that the image has been processed and the data stored. He then accesses an MS-SQL® database through an ODBC connected Excel® spreadsheet with email and, after a few minutes, receives a response. Finally, he prints out a full-color, 150-page report on his hi-tech, miniaturized LaserJet® printer, turns to the cowboy and says, "You have exactly 1,586 cows and calves."

"That's right. Well, I guess you can take one of my calves," says Bud.

He watches the young man select one of the animals and looks on with amusement as the young man stuffs it into the trunk of his car.

Then Bud says to the young man, "Hey, if I can tell you exactly what your business is, will you give me back my calf?"

The young man thinks about it for a second and then says, "Okay, why not?"

"You're a Congressman for the U.S. Government", says Bud.

"Wow! That's correct," says the yuppie, "but how did you guess that?"

"No guessing required." answered the cowboy. "You showed up here even though nobody called you; you want to get paid for an answer I already knew, to a question I never asked. You used millions of dollars worth of equipment trying to show me how much smarter than me you are; and you don't know a thing about how working people make a living – or about cows, for that matter. This is a herd of sheep........ Now, give me back my dog.

Psychology and Life

Amazing!

This ia amazing! Occdrnig to a rscheearch at Cmabrigde Uinervtisy, it deosn't mttaer in
waht oredr the ltteers in a wrod are, the olny iprmoetnt tihng is taht the frist and lsat ltteer be at the rghit pclae. The rset can be a total mses and you can sitll raed it wouthit porbelm.

Tihs is bcuseae the huamn mnid deos not raed ervey lteter by istlef, but the wrod as a wlohe.

Amzanig huh?

Chicken

Man runs to the doctor and says, "Doctor, you've got to help me. My wife thinks she's a chicken"

Doctor says, "How long has she had this condition?"

"Two years," says the man.

"Then why did it take you so long to come and see me?'

The man shrugs his shoulders, "we needed the eggs."

Christmas Carols for the Psychiatrically Challenged

Schizophrenia --- Do You Hear What I Hear?

Multiple Personality Disorder --- We Three Queens Disoriented Are

Dementia --- I Think I'll be Home for Christmas

Narcissistic --- Hark the Herald Angles Sing About Me

Manic --- Deck the Halls and Walls and House and Lawn and Streets and Stores and Office and

Town and Cars and Busses and Trucks and trees and Fire Hydrants and......

Paranoid --- Santa Claus is Coming to Get me

Borderline Personality Disorder --- Thoughts of Roasting on an Open Fire

Personality Disorder --- You Better Watch Out, I'm Gonna Cry, I'm Gonna Pout, Maybe I'll tell You Why

Obsessive Compulsive Disorder ---Jingle Bells, jingle Bells, Jingle Bells, Jingle Bells, Jingle Bells, Jingle Bells, Jingle Bells, Jingle Bells, Jingle Bells

Mental Evaluation

During a visit to the mental asylum, a visitor asked the Director how you determine whether or not a patient should be institutionalized.

"Well," said the Director, "we fill up a bathtub, then, we offer a teaspoon, a teacup and a bucket to the patient and ask him or her to empty the bathtub."

"Oh, I understand," said the visitor. "A normal person would use the bucket because it's bigger than the spoon or the teacup."

"No" said the Director, "A normal person would pull the plug.

"Do you want a bed near the window?"

Move Over

A psychiatrist visited a California mental institution and asked a patient, "How did you get here? What was the nature of your illness?" He got the following reply.

"Well, it all started when I got married and I guess I should never have done it. I married a widow with a grown daughter who then became my stepdaughter.

"My dad came to visit us, fell in love with my lovely stepdaughter, then married her. And so my stepdaughter was now my stepmother.

Soon, my wife had a son who was, of course, my daddy's brother-in-law since he is the half-brother of my stepdaughter, who is now, of course, my daddy's wife.

"So, as I told you, when my stepdaughter married my daddy, she was at once my stepmother! Now, since my new son is brother to my stepmother, he also became my uncle. As you know, my wife is my step-grandmother since she is my stepmother's mother. Don't forget that my stepmother is my stepdaughter. Remember, too, that I am my wife's grandson.

"But hold on just a few minutes more. You see, since I'm married to my step-grandmother, I am not only the wife's grandson and her hubby, but I am also my own grandfather.

Now can you understand how I got put in this place?"

After staring blankly with a dizzy look on his face, the psychiatrist replied: "Move over!

Religion, Church and Faith

Atheist and the Little Girl

An atheist was seated next to a little girl on an airplane and he turned to her and said, "Do you want to talk? Flights go quicker if you strike up a conversation with your fellow passenger."

The little girl, who had just started to read her book, replied to the total stranger, "What would you want to talk about?"

Oh, I don't know," said the atheist. "How about why there is no God, or no Heaven or Hell, or no life after death?" as he smiled smugly.

"OK," she said. "Those could be interesting topics but let me ask you a question first. A horse, a cow, and a deer all eat the same stuff - grass. Yet a deer excretes little pellets, while a cow turns out a flat patty, but a horse produces clumps. Why do you suppose that is?"

The atheist, visibly surprised by the little girl's intelligence, thinks about it and says, "Hmmm, I have no idea."

To which the little girl replies, "Do you really feel qualified to discuss why there is no God, or no Heaven or Hell, or no life after death, when you don't know poop?" And then she went back to reading her book.

Bears Chapel

The story is told that the 1985 Chicago Bears would have a chapel service each Sunday morning before games.

One week, Coach Mike Ditka called on William "Refrigerator" Perry to lead in the Lord's Prayer.

Jim McMann leaned over to the Chaplain who was seated next to him and whispered, "Watch this. This is going to be rich!. Fridge doesn't know the Lord's Prayer."

The chaplain said, "Oh, I bet he does."

McMann countered, "I bet you 50 bucks that he doesn't".

The chaplain agreed to take the bet.

Perry began, "Now I lay me down to sleep…"

McMann disgustedly reached in his pocket and gave the chaplain $50, and muttered, "I never would have thought he would have known that!"

Biblical Baseball

Baseball was a well-established sport even in biblical times.:

Genesis 1:1 ... "In the big inning"

Genesis 24: ... 15,16 "Rebekah went to the well with a pitcher"

Numbers 11:32 ... "ten homers"

Second Kings 25:16 ... "and the bases which Solomon had made"

Psalms 19:12 ... "Who can understand his errors?"

Psalms 26:1 ... "1 have trusted, therefore, I shall not slide."

Jeremiah 15:7 ... "And I will fan them"

Ezekiel 36:12 ... "Yea, I will cause men to walk"

Luke 17:17 ... "but where are the nine?"

Galatians 5:7 ... "Ye did run well"

Biblical Headlines

If Biblical headlines were written by today's media:

On the Red Sea crossing:
WETLANDS TRAMPLED IN LABOR STRIKE

Pursuing Environmentalists Killed

On David vs. Goliath:
HATE CRIME KILLS BELOVED CHAMPION
Psychologist Questions Influence of Rock

On Elijah on Mt. Carmel
FIRE SENDS RELIGIOUS RIGHT EXTREMIST INTO FRENZY
400 Killed

On the birth of Christ:
HOTELS FULL, ANIMALS LEFT HOMELESS
Animal Rights Activists Enraged by Insensitive Couple

On feeding the 5,000:
PREACHER STEALS CHILD'S LUNCH
Disciples Mystified Over Behavior

On healing the 10 lepers:
LOCAL DOCTOR'S PRACTICE RUINED
"Faith Healer" Causes Bankruptcy

On healing of the Nazarene demoniac:
MADMAN'S FRIEND CAUSES STAMPEDE
Local Farmer's Investment Lost

On raising Lazarus from the dead:
FUNDAMENTALIST PREACHER RAISES A STINK
Reading of will to be Delayed

Can of Worms- Check Your Assumptions

Sometimes conclusions aren't as obvious as they might seem:

A minister decided that a visual demonstration would add emphasis to his Sunday sermon. Four worms were placed into four separate jars.

The first worm was put into a container of alcohol.

The second worm was put into a container of cigarette smoke.

The third worm was put into a container of chocolate syrup.

The fourth worm was put into a container of good clean soil.

At the conclusion of the sermon, the Minister reported the following results:

The first worm in alcohol - Dead.

The second worm in cigarette smoke - Dead.

Third worm in chocolate syrup - Dead.

Fourth worm in good clean soil - Alive.

So the Minister asked the congregation - What can you learn from this demonstration?

A little old woman in the back quickly raised her hand and said, "As long as you drink, smoke and eat chocolate, you won't have worms!"

Christian Example

The light turned yellow, just in front of him. He did the right thing, stopping at the crosswalk, even though he could have beaten the red light by accelerating through the intersection.

The tailgating woman was furious and honked her horn, screaming in frustration, as she missed her chance to get through the intersection, dropping her cell phone and makeup. As she was still in mid-rant, she heard a tap on her window and looked up into the face of a very serious police officer. The officer ordered her to exit her car with her hands up. He took her to the police station where she was searched fingerprinted, photographed, and placed in a holding cell.

After a couple of hours, a policeman approached the cell and opened the door. She was escorted back to the booking desk where the arresting officer was waiting with her personal effects.

He said, "I'm very sorry for this mistake. You see, I pulled up behind your car while you were blowing your horn, flipping off the guy in front of you and cussing a blue streak at him. I noticed the 'What Would Jesus Do' bumper sticker, the 'Choose Life' license plate holder, the 'Follow Me to Sunday-School' bumper sticker, and the chrome-plated Christian fish emblem on the trunk, so naturally...I assumed you had stolen the car."

Clear Words

At the Sunday morning church service, the minister asked if anyone in the congregation would like to express praise for answered prayers.

A lady stood and walked to the podium. She said, "I have a Praise. Two months ago, my husband, Tom, had a terrible bicycle crash and his scrotum was completely crushed. The pain was terrible and the doctors didn't know if they could help him."

You could hear a muffled gasp from all the men in the congregation as they imagined the pain that poor Tom must have experienced.

"Tom was unable to hold me or the children," she went on, "and every movement caused him terrible pain. We prayed as the doctors performed a very delicate operation, which lasted for over five hours, and it turned out they were able to piece together the crushed remnants of Tom's scrotum, and wrap wire around it to hold it in place."

Again, the men in the congregation were unnerved and squirmed uncomfortably as they imagined the horrible surgery that was performed on Tom.

"Now," she announced in a quavering voice, "thank the Lord, after six weeks, Tom is now out of the hospital and the doctors say that with time, his scrotum should recover completely."

All the men sighed with relief.

The minister rose and tentatively asked if anyone else had

something to say. A man stood up and walked slowly to the podium.

He said, "I'm Tom." The entire congregation held its breath. "I just want to tell my wife that the word is sternum."

Deep Question

How Many Does it Take to Change a Lightbulb?

Charismatics: Only one. Hands are already in the air.

Pentecostals: Ten. One to change the bulb, nine to pray against the spirit of darkness.

Presbyterians: None. Lights will go on and off at predestined times.

Roman Catholic: None. Candles only.

Baptists: At least 15. One to change the light bulb and three committees to approve the change and decide who brings the *potato salad & fried chicken.*

Episcopalians: Three. One to call the electrician, one to mix the drinks and one to talk about how much better the old bulb was.

Mormons: Five. One man to change the bulb and four wives to tell him how to do it.

Unitarians: We choose not to make a statement, either in favor of or against the need for a light bulb. However, if in your own journey you have found that light bulbs work for you, that is fine. You are invited to write a poem or compose a modern dance about your light bulb for the next Sunday service, in which we will explore the number of light bulb traditions, including incandescent, fluorescent, three-way, long-life and tinted, all of which are equally valid paths to luminescence.

Methodists: Undetermined. Whether your light is bright, dull or completely out, you are loved. You can be a light bulb, turnip bulb or tulip bulb. Church wide lighting service is planned for Sunday. Bring bulb of your choice and a covered dish.

Nazarene: Six. One woman to replace the bulb while five men review the church lighting policy.

Lutherans: None. Lutherans don't believe in change.

Amish: What's a light bulb??

Deserted Island

Two men crashed in their private plane on a South Pacific Island. Both survived. One of the men brushed himself off and then proceeded to run all over the island to see if they had any chance of survival. When he returned, he rushed up to the other man and screamed, "This island is uninhabited, there is no food, there is no water. We are going to die!"

The other man leaned back against the fuselage of the wrecked plane,
folded his arms and responded, "No we're not. I make over $250,000 a week."

The first man grabbed his friend and shook him. "Listen, we are on an uninhabited island. There is no food, no water. We are going to die!"

The other man, unruffled, again responded. "No, I make over $250,000 a week."

Mystified, the first man, taken aback with such an answer again repeated, "For the last time, I'm telling you we ARE doomed. There is NO one else on this island. There is NO food. There is NO water. We are, I repeat, going to die a slow death."

Still unfazed, the first man looked the other in the eyes and said, "Do not make me say this again. I make over $250,000 per week, I am a Baptist, and I tithe. MY PASTOR WILL FIND US!"

For the Baptists?

A Methodist minister meets three Baptist deacons on the golf course and invites them to come to his church some Sunday. Not too many weeks thereafter and just as services are starting, they show up. Attendance was good in the church and there wasn't a pew available. Several church members were already seated on folding chairs. When the minister, just starting the service, saw the three Baptist deacons enter, he leaned down from the pulpit and whispered to the nearest usher, "Please get three chairs for my Baptist friends in the back."

The usher, hard of hearing, leaned closer and said, "I beg your pardon?"

"Get three chairs for my Baptist friends," repeated the minister. The usher strained closer with a puzzled look still on his face.

Once more the minister tried, speaking slowly and distinctly. "Three chairs. For the Baptists," he enunciated.

The usher's face lit up in comprehension, and he turned to face the congregation. "All right, everybody," he called out to the assembled worshipers. "Three cheers for the Baptists!"

Graveside Manner

The bagpiper was asked by a funeral director to play at a grave-side service for a homeless man. He had no family or friends, so the service was to be at a pauper's cemetery in the Kentucky back-country. Not being familiar with the backwoods, the bagpiper got lost and finally arrived an hour late. He saw the funeral guy had evidently gone and the hearse was nowhere in sight.

There were only the diggers and crew left and they were eating lunch. He felt badly and apologized to the men for being late. He then went to the side of the grave and looking down saw that the vault lid was already in place. Not knowing what else to do, he started to play.

The workers put down their lunches and began to gather around. He played out his heart and soul for this man with no family and friends. He played like never before for this poor homeless man. As he played "Amazing Grace" the workers began to weep. He began to weep too. When he finished playing, he packed up his bagpipes and started for his car, with his head hung low and his heart full.

As he was opening the door to his car, he heard one of the workers say, "Sweet Jesus, I never seen nothin' like that before... and I've been putting in septic tanks for over twenty years."

How Faiths Fight Fires

Recently, just as an ecumenical gathering was commencing, a secretary rushed in shouting, "The building is on fire!"

The Methodists gathered in a corner and prayed.

The Baptists cried, "Where is the water?"

The Quakers quietly praised God for blessings that fire brings.

The Lutherans posted a notice on the door declaring that fire was evil.

The Roman Catholics passed the plate to cover the damage.

The Jews posted symbols on the doors hoping the fire would pass.

The Congregationalists shouted, "Every man for himself."

The Fundamentalists proclaimed, "It's the vengeance of God!"

The Episcopalians formed a procession and marched out.

The Christian Scientists concluded that the fire would burn itself out.

The Presbyterians appointed a chairperson, who was to appoint a committee to look into the matter and submit a written report.

The Unity Students proclaimed the fire had no power over them.

Some Atheists in attendance didn't believe there was a fire.

The Secretary grabbed the fire extinguisher and put out the fire.

It's a Miracle!

Sister Mary Ann, who worked for a home health agency, was out making her rounds visiting homebound patients. When she ran out of gas. As luck would have it, an Exxon Gasoline station was just a block away. She walked to the station to borrow a gas can and buy some gas.

The attendant told her that the only gas can he owned had been loaned out, but she could wait until It was returned.

Since Sister Mary Ann was on the way to see a patient, she decided not to wait and walked Back to her car. She looked for something in her car that she could fill with gas and spotted the bedpan she was taking to the patient. Always resourceful, Sister Mary Ann Carried the bedpan to the station, filled it with Gasoline, and carried the full bedpan back to her car. As she was pouring the gas into her tank, two Baptists watched from across the street.

One of them turned to the other and said, "If it starts, I'm turning Catholic."

Jesus was......

My Cajun friend swears that Jesus was a Cajun:

1. He liked to serve fish to his friends.

2. He could make his own wine.

3. And he wasn't afraid of water.

My black friend had 3 good arguments that Jesus was Black:

1. He called everyone "brother".

2. He liked Gospel.

3. He couldn't get a fair trial.

My Jewish friend had 3 equally good arguments that Jesus was Jewish:

1. He went into His Father's business.

2. He lived at home until he was 30.

3. He was sure his Mother was a virgin and his mother was sure he was God.

My Italian friend gave his 3 equally good arguments that Jesus was Italian:

1. He talked with his hands.

2. He had wine with every meal.

3. He used olive oil.

My California friends also had 3 equally good arguments that Jesus was a Californian:

1. He never cut his hair.

2. He walked around barefoot all the time.

3. He started a new religion.

My Irish friend then gave his 3 equally good arguments that Jesus was Irish:

1. He never got married.

2. He was always telling stories.

3. He loved green pastures.

But my lady friend had the most compelling evidence of all that Jesus was a woman:

1. He fed a crowd at a moment's notice when there was no food.

2. He kept trying to get a message across to a bunch of men who just didn't get it.

3. And even when he was dead, he had to get up because there was more work to do.

Last Rites

A Catholic man is struck by a bus on a busy street. He is lying near death on the sidewalk as a crowd gathers. "A preacher, somebody get me a preacher!" the man gasps. Minutes drag on and no one steps out of the crowd.

A policeman checks the crowd and finally yells, "A PRIEST, PLEASE! Isn't there a priest in this crowd to give this man his last rites?"

Finally, out of the crowd steps a little old Jewish man of at least 80 years of age. "Mr. Policeman," says the man, "I'm not a priest. I'm not even a Christian. But for 50 years now I'm living behind the Catholic Church on First Avenue, and every night I'm overhearing their services. I can recall a lot of it, and maybe I can be of some comfort to this poor man."

The policeman agrees, and clears the crowd so the man can get through to where the injured man lay.

The old Jewish man kneels down, leans over the prostrate man and says in a solemn voice: "B-4, I-19, N-38, G-54, O-72..."

Mysterious Ways

There was a pastor of a church who had a kitten that climbed up a tree in his backyard and then was afraid to come down. The pastor coaxed, offered warm milk, etc., but the kitty would not come down. The tree was not sturdy enough to climb, so the pastor decided that if he tied a rope to his car and drove away so that the tree bent down, he could then reach up and get the kitten. He did! All the while, checking his progress in the car frequently, then figured if he went just a little bit further, the tree would be bent sufficiently for him to reach the kitten. But as he moved a little further forward, the rope broke. The tree went "boing!" and the kitten instantly sailed through the air-out of sight.

The pastor felt terrible. He walked all over the neighborhood asking people if they'd seen a little kitten. No. Nobody had seen a stray kitten. So he prayed, "Lord, I just commit this kitten to your keeping," and went on about his business.

A few days later he was at the grocery store, and met one of his church members. He happened to look into her shopping cart and was amazed to see cat food. Now this woman was a cat hater and everyone knew it, so he asked her, "Why are you buying cat food when you hate cats so much?"

She replied, "You won't believe this," and told him how her little girl had been begging her for a cat, but she kept refusing.

Then a few days before, the child had begged again, so the Mom finally told her little girl, "Well, if God gives you a cat, I'll let you keep it?"

She told the pastor, "I watched my child go out in the yard, get on her knees, and ask God for a cat. And really, Pastor, you won't believe this, but I saw it with my own eyes. A kitten suddenly came flying out of the blue sky, with its paws outspread, and landed right in front of her."

Never underestimate the Power of God and His unique sense of humor.

No Reason to be scared

One bright, beautiful Sunday morning, everyone in tiny Smithville wakes up early and goes to their local church. Before the service starts, the townspeople sit in their pews and talk about their lives, their families, etc.

Suddenly, at the altar, Satan appears!! Everyone starts screaming and running for the front entrance, trampling each other in their determined efforts to get away from Evil Incarnate.

Soon, everyone is evacuated from the church except for one man, who sits calmly in his pew, seemingly oblivious to the fact that God's ultimate enemy is in his presence. This confuses Satan a bit.

Satan walks up to the man and says, "Hey, don't you know who I am?"

The man says, "Yep, sure do."

Satan says, "Well, aren't you afraid of me?"

The man says, "Nope, sure ain't."

Satan, perturbed, says, "And why aren't you afraid of me?"

"Well, I've been married to your sister for 25 years."

Not-so-Subtle Warning

Reverend Boudreaux was the part-time pastor of the local Cajun Baptist Church and Pastor Thibodaux was the minister of the Covenant Church across the road. They were both standing by the road, pounding a sign into the ground that read:

'Da End is Near
Turn Yo Sef 'Roun Now
Afore It Be Too Late!'

As a car sped past them, the driver leaned out his window and yelled, 'You religious nuts!' From the curve they heard screeching tires, and a big splash...

Boudreaux turns to ole Thibodaux and asks, 'Do ya tink maybe da sign should jus say...
'Bridge Out?'

Once a Baptist- Always a Baptist

John Smith was the only Protestant to move into a large Catholic neighborhood. On the first Friday of Lent, John was outside grilling a big juicy steak on his grill. Meanwhile, all of his neighbors were eating cold tuna fish for supper. This went on each Friday of Lent. On the last Friday of Lent, the neighborhood men got together and decided that something had to be done about John, he was tempting them to eat meat each Friday of Lent, and they couldn't take it anymore.

They decided to try and convert John to be a Catholic. They went over and talked to him and were so happy that he decided to join all of his neighbors and become a Catholic.

They took him to church, and the Priest sprinkled some water over him and said, "You were born a Baptist, you were raised a Baptist, and now you are Catholic." The men were so relieved, now their biggest Lenten temptation was resolved.

The next year's Lenten season rolled around. The first Friday of Lent came, and just at supper time, when the neighborhood was sitting down to their tuna fish dinner, came the wafting smell of steak cooking on a grill. The neighborhood men could not believe their noses! WHAT WAS GOING ON?

They called each other up and decided to meet over in John's yard to see if he had forgotten it was the first Friday of Lent?

The group arrived just in time to see John standing over his grill with a small pitcher of water. He was sprinkling some water over his steak on the grill, saying, "You were born a cow, you were raised a cow, and now you are a fish."

Pavement?

There once was a rich man who was near death. He was very grieved because he had worked so hard for his money and he wanted to be able to take it with him to heaven. So he began to pray that he might be able to take some of his wealth with him.

An angel hears his plea and appears to him, "Sorry, but you can't take your wealth with you."

The man implores the angel to speak to God to see if He might bend the rules.
The man continues to pray that his wealth could follow him. The angel reappears and informs the man that God has decided to allow him to take one suitcase with him. Overjoyed, the man gathers his largest suitcase and fills it with pure gold bars and places it beside his bed.

Soon afterward the man dies and shows up at the Gates of Heaven to greet St. Peter. Seeing the suitcase Peter says, "Hold on, you can't bring that in here!"

But the man explains to him that he has permission and asks him to verify his story with the Lord. Sure enough, Peter checks and comes back saying, "You're right. You are allowed one carry-on bag, but I'm supposed to check its contents before letting it through."

Peter opens the suitcase to inspect the worldly items that the man found too precious to leave behind and exclaims, "You brought pavement?!?!"

Prayer Ministry

The small country church had a really active prayer ministry. On Sunday night they developed a tradition of holding a special prayer service that attracted people from all over the county At the end of the service one night the preacher called out, "Anyone here with 'special needs' who wants to be prayed over, please come forward to the altar."

With that, a young man wearing bib overalls got in line. He appeared a bit nervous. When it was his turn, the Preacher asked, "Son, what do you want us to pray about for you?"

Rather reluctantly the young man replied, "Preacher, I need you to pray for help with my hearing."

Ready to get to work, the preacher put a finger of one hand in the young man's ear, placed his other hand on top of the boy's head, and then commenced to pray in a mighty way. He prayed and prayed and prayed. He prayed a "blue streak" for almost 15 minutes. The congregation joined in with great enthusiasm.

After winding down the prayer the preacher removed his hands, stood back and asked, "Son, how is your hearing now?"

The young man answered, "I don't know, sir. My lawyer said the judge scheduled it for next Thursday."

Proper Burial

Unable to attend the funeral after his Uncle Charlie died, a man who lived far away called his brother and told him, "Do something nice for Uncle Charlie and send me the bill."

Later, he got a bill for $200.00, which he paid. The next month, he got another bill for $200.00, which he also paid, figuring it was some incidental expense. But, when the bills for $200.00 kept arriving every month, he finally called his brother again to find out what was going on.

"Well," said the other brother, "You said to do something nice for Uncle Charlie. So I rented him a tuxedo."

Repentant Parrot

Mary received a parrot as a gift. The parrot was fully grown with a very bad attitude and worse vocabulary. Every other word was a curse: those that weren't curses were to say the least, rude. Mary tried to change the bird's attitude by constantly saying polite things. Words and playing soft music– anything she could think of. Nothing worked. She yelled at the bird and the bird got worse. She shook the bird and the bird got madder and more rude.

Finally, in a moment of desperation, Mary put the parrot in the freezer to get a minute of peace. For a few moments she heard the bird swearing, squawking kicking and screaming and then, suddenly there was absolute quiet.

Mary was frightened that she might have actually hurt the bird and quickly opened the freezer door.

The parrot calmly stepped out onto Mary's extended arm and said: "I'm very sorry that I offended you with my language and my actions and I ask your forgiveness. I will endeavor to correct my behavior and I am sure it will never happen again."

Mary was astounded at the changes in the bird's attitude and was about to ask what had changed him, when the parrot continued, "May I ask what the chicken did?"

Sample Sermon

The pastor put sanitary hot air hand dryers in the rest rooms at his church and after two weeks, took them out.

When asked why, he confessed that they worked fine, but when he went in there, he saw a sign that read, "For a sample of this week's sermon, push the button."

Self- Control

A Pastor was playing golf with 3 laymen. When the laymen would miss a shot, they would all grumble and curse in frustration. With the Pastor, on the other hand, no matter how bad the shot never changed his demeanor.

"How do you have such control?", asked one of the laymen.

"Actually, I mask it fairly well", said the Pastor. "Perhaps you haven't noticed, but where I spit, the grass never grows again."

Self- sufficient, Really

One day a group of scientists got together and decided that man had come a long way and no longer needed God. So they picked one scientist to go and tell Him that they were done with Him.

The scientist walked up to God and said, "God, we've decided that we no longer need you. We're to the point that we can clone people and do many miraculous things, so why don't you just go on and get lost."

He listened very patiently and kindly to the man and after the scientist was done talking, God said, "Very well, how about this, let's say we have a man making contest."

To which the scientist replied, "OK, great!"

But God added, "Now, we're going to do this just like I did back in the old days with Adam."

The scientist said, "Sure, no problem" and bent down and grabbed himself a handful of dirt.

God just looked at him and said, "No, no, no. You go get your own dirt!"

Staff Aptitude

MEMORANDUM

TO: Jesus, Son of Joseph, Woodcrafters shop, Nazareth

FROM: Jordan Management Consultants, Jerusalem

SUBJECT: Staff Aptitude Test.

DATE: March 29, 30 A.D.

Thank you for submitting the resumes of the 12 men you picked for management positions in your new organization. All of them have now taken our battery of tests, and we have not only run the results through our computer but also have arranged personal interviews for each of them with our psychologist and vocational consultant. It is the staff opinion that most of your nominees are lacking in background, education and vocational aptitude for the type of enterprise you are undertaking. They do not have the team concept. We would recommend that you continue your search for persons of experience in managerial ability and proven capability.

Simon Peter is emotionally unstable and given to fits of temper.

Andrew has absolutely no qualities of leadership.

The two brothers, James and John, the sons of Zebedee, place personal interest above company loyalty.

Thomas demonstrates a questioning attitude that would tend to undermine morale.

We feel that it is our duty to tell you that Matthew has been blacklisted by the Greater Jerusalem Better Business Bureau.

James, the son of Alphaeus, and Thaddeus definitely have radical leanings, and they both registered a high score on the manic-depressive scale.

One of the candidates, however, shows great potential. He is a man of ability and resourcefulness, meets people well, has a keen business mind and has contact in high places. He is highly motivated, ambitious and innovative. We recommend Judas Iscariot as your controller and right- hand man. All other profiles are self-explanatory. We wish you every success in your new venture.

Sincerely, Jordan Management Consultants

Texas Beer Joint Sues Church

In Mt. Vernon, Texas, Drummond's Bar began construction on a new building to increase their business. In response, the local Baptist church started a campaign to block the bar from opening with petitions and prayers. Work progressed right up until the week before opening when lightning struck the bar and it burned to the ground.

The church folks were rather smug in their outlook after that, until the bar owner sued the church on the grounds that the church was ultimately responsible for the demise of his building, either through direct or indirect actions or means.

In its reply to the court, the church vehemently denied all responsibility or any connection to the building's demise.

The judge read through the plaintiff's complaint and the defendant's reply and at the opening hearing he commented, "I don't know how I'm going to decide this, but it appears from the paperwork that we have a bar owner who believes in the power of prayer, and an entire church congregation that does not."

Texas Church Test

An old Texan went to the local church and asked to join. The preacher said, 'OK, but you have to pass a small Bible test first.'

The first Question is 'Where was Jesus born?'

The man answered, 'Longview.'

The preacher said. 'Sorry...you can't join our church.'

So....he went to another church and asked to join.

The preacher said, 'We would love to have you, but you have to pass a Bible test first.

Where was Jesus born?'

The man said. 'Tyler.'

The preacher said, 'Sorry...you can't join our church.'

So....he goes to another church and asks, to join.

The preacher said, 'That's great; we welcome you with open arms.'

The man said, 'I don't have to pass no Bible test first?'

The preacher said, 'No.'

The man said, 'Can I ask you a question?'

The preacher said, 'Sure.'

The man said, 'Where was Jesus born?'

The preacher said, 'Palestine.'

The man mumbled to himself, 'I knew it was in East Texas somewhere.'

The Cowboy

A cowboy in west Texas came off the range to go to church. His jeans, shirt and boots were clean and neat and he had a well-worn Bible in his hand. Still, he was a bit out of place- the other men had on suits and ties and the women wore fancy dresses. The service went well enough, and afterwards the pastor was greeting all of the worshippers at the rear of the church.

When the cowboy came through the line, the pastor said." We're sure glad to have you here today. Next time, though, before you come let me ask you to do something. Pray to God and ask Him what the appropriate attire would be to come to worship here."

About six weeks later the cowboy was once again off the range, and he went to the same church. Once again, his jeans, shirt and boots were clean and neat and he had a well-worn Bible in his hand. This time, the pastor spotted him as he came in, and immediately went to him.

"I thought I told you to pray to God and ask Him what you should wear to this church."

"Oh, I did", said the cowboy.

"What did He say?" asked the Pastor.

"Oh", said the Cowboy, "He said that He didn't have a clue. Said that He's never been here before."

The Prodigal Son - in the Key of F

Feeling footloose and frisky a feather-brained fellow forced his fond father to fork over the family finances. He flew far to foreign fields and frittered his fortune feasting fabulously with faithless friends.

Finally facing famine and fleeced by his fellows in folly, he found himself a feed-flinger in a filthy farmyard. Fairly famished he fain would have filled his frame with the foraged foods of the fodder fragments left by the filthy farmyard creatures.

"Fooey", he said, "My father's flunkies fare far fancier," the frazzled fugitive found feverishly, frankly facing facts.

Frustrated by failure and filled with foreboding he forthwith fled to his family. Falling at his father's feet, he floundered forlornly. "Father, I have flunked and fruitlessly forfeited family favour."

But the faithful father, forestalling further flinching frantically flagged the flunkies. "Fetch forth the finest fatling and fix a feast."

But the fugitive's fault-finding frater frowned on the fickle forgiveness of the former folderol. His fury flashed. But fussing was futile, for the far-sighted father figured, such filial fidelity is fine, but what forbids fervent festivity.

The fugitive is found. "Unfurl the flags, with fanfares flaring, let fun and frolic freely flow. Former failure is forgotten, folly forsaken, forgiveness forms the foundation for future fortitude."

(Author Unknown) - but it must be someone with a lot of time on their hands

The Real Thing

The pastor of a church was taking his first trip away on a Sunday, and he asked another pastor to come in and preach the service for him. The substitute pastor agreed to come. He was quite young, just out of seminary, and this was his first time preaching.

When he got up to speak on Sunday, he tried to explain to the congregation why he'd come, and give them some comfort about it. He pointed up to the stained- glass windows to illustrate this. "You see where there's a missing pane, and there's a piece of cardboard over it? That's sort of what I'm doing. I'm just filling in the space until your pastor returns."

He went on about this a little bit, then went into his sermon. The young substitute pastor gave a wonderful, inspired talk that Sunday.

After the service, a lovely old woman came up to him, took his hand, and said, "Pastor, don't you ever let anyone say that you're like that piece of cardboard. Believe me, you are the real pane!"

Turkey Confession

Ducking into confession with a turkey in his arms, Brian said, "Forgive me, Father, for I have sinned. I stole this turkey to feed my family. Would you take it and settle my guilt?"

"Certainly not," said the Priest. "As penance, you must return it to the one from whom you stole it."

"I tried," Brian sobbed, "but he refused. Oh, Father, what should I do?"

"If what you say is true, then it is all right for you to keep it for your family."

Thanking the Priest, Brian hurried off. When confession was over, the Priest returned to his residence. When he walked into the kitchen, he found that someone had stolen his turkey.

Three Huts

A man was stranded on the proverbial deserted Pacific island for years. Finally, one day a boat comes sailing into view, and the man frantically waves and draws the skipper's attention. The boat comes near the island and the sailor gets out and greets the stranded man.

After awhile the sailor asks, "What are those three huts you have here?"

"Well, that's my house there."

"What's that next hut?" asks the sailor.

"I built that hut to be my church."

"What about the other hut?"

"Oh, that's where I used to go to church."

Sports

Amazing Race

Some race horses staying in a stable. One of them starts to boast about his track record. "In the last 15 races, I've won 8 of them!"

Another horse breaks in, "Well in the last 27 races, I've won 19!!"

"Oh, that's good, but in the last 36 races, I've one 28!" says another, flicking his tail.

At this point, they notice that a greyhound dog has been sitting there listening. "I don't mean to boast," says the greyhound, "but in MY last 90 races, I've won 88 of them!" The horses are clearly amazed.

"Wow!" says one, after a hushed silence. "A talking dog."

Avid Baseball Fan

The world's most avid baseball fan had arrived at the stadium for the first game of the World Series only to realize he had left his ticket at home. Not wanting to miss any of the first inning, he went to the ticket booth and got in a long line to work things out.

After an hour's wait, he was just a few feet from the booth when a voice called out, 'Hey Dave!'

The fan looked up, stepped out of line and tried to find the owner of the voice- with no success. Then he realized he had lost his place in line and had to wait all over again.

When the fan finally got his ticket, he was thirsty, so he went to buy a drink. The line at the concessions stand was long, too, but since the game hadn't started he decided to wait.

Just as he got to the window, a voice called out, Hey Dave!"

Again, the fan tried to find the voice- but no luck. He was very upset as he got back in line for his drink.

Finally, the fan went to his seat, eager for the game to begin. As he waited for the first pitch, he heard the voice calling, "Hey Dave!" once more.

Furious, he stood up and yelled at the top of his lungs, "MY NAME IS NOT DAVE!

Baseball in Heaven?

Two buddies Bob and Earl were two of the biggest baseball fans in America. Their entire adult lives, Bob and Earl discussed baseball history in winter, and they pored over every box score during the season. They went 60 or more games a year. They even agreed that whoever died first would try to come back and tell the other if there was baseball in heaven.

One summer night, Bob passed way in his sleep after watching the Yankee victory earlier in the evening. He died happy. A few nights later, his buddy Earl awoke to the sound of Bob's voice from beyond.

"Bob, is that you?" Earl asked.

"Of course it's me" Bob replied.

"This is unbelievable!" exclaimed Earl. "So tell me, is there baseball in heaven?"

"Well I have some good news and some bad news for you. Which do you want to hear first?"

"Well, the good news is that yes there is baseball in heaven, Earl."

"Oh, that is wonderful. So what could possibly be the bad news?"

"You're pitching tomorrow night!"

Blind Ambition

Charlie Boswell has inspired thousands to rise above circumstances and live their true passion. Charlie was blinded during World War II while rescuing his friend from a tank that was under fire. He was a great athlete before his accident and in a testimony to his talent and determination he decided to try a brand- new sport, a sport he never imagined playing, even with his eyesight . . .golf!

Through determination and a deep love for the game he became the National Blind Golf Champion! He won that honor 13 times. One of his heroes was the great golfer Ben Hogan, so it truly was an honor for Charlie to win the Ben Hogan Award in 1958.

Upon meeting Ben Hogan, Charlie was awestruck and stated that he had one wish and it was to have one round of golf with the great Ben Hogan. Mr. Hogan agreed that playing a round together would be an honor for him as well, as he had heard about all of Charlie's accomplishments and truly admired his skills.

"Would you like to play for money, Mr. Hogan?" blurted out Charlie.

"I can't play you for money, it wouldn't be fair!" said Mr.Hogan.

"Aw, come on, Mr. Hogan...$1,000 per hole!"

"I can't, what would people think of me, taking advantage of you and your circumstance," replied the sighted golfer.

"Chicken, Mr. Hogan?"

"Okay," blurted a frustrated Hogan, "but I am going to play my best!"

"I wouldn't expect anything else," said the confident Boswell.

"You're on Mr. Boswell, you name the time and the place!"

A very self-assured Boswell responded "10 o'clock . . . tonight!"

Blond Fishing

A blond was stopped by a game warden recently with two ice chests full of fish. She was leaving a cove well-known for its fishing.

The game warden asked her, "Do you have a license to catch those fish?"

"No, sir", she replied, "I don't have a license. But these are my pet fish."

"Pet fish?"

"Yes sir. Every night, I take these here fish down to the lake and let 'em swim 'round for awhile. Then, when I whistle, they jump right back into these ice chests and I take 'em home."

"That's a bunch of hooey! Fish can't do that."

The blond looked at the warden and then said, "It's the truth. It really works."

"O. K.", said the warden. "I've got to see this!"

The blond poured the fish into the lake and stood and waited.

After several minutes, the warden says, "Well?"

"Well, what?", said the blond.

The warden says, "When are you going to call them back?"

"Call who back?"

"The FISH", replied the warden!

"What fish?", replied the blond.

.... And you thought blonds were supposed to be dumb?

Deep Hole

Two rednecks are out hunting, and as they are walking along, they come upon a huge hole in the ground. They approach it and are amazed by the size of it.

The first hunter says, "Wow, that's some hole, I can't even see the bottom. I wonder how deep it is?"

The second hunter says "I don't know, let's throw something down and listen and see how long hit takes to hit bottom."

The first hunter says, "There's this old transmission here, give me a hand and we'll throw it in and see."

So they pick it up, carry it over, count one, and two and three, and throw it in the hole. They are standing there listening and looking over the edge and they hear a rustling in the brush behind them. As they turn around, they see a goat come crashing through the brush, run up to the hole with no hesitation, and jump in headfirst.

While they are standing there looking at each other, looking in the hole, and trying to figure out what that was all about, an old farmer walks up.

"Say there", says the farmer, "you fellers didn't happen to see my goat around here anywhere, did you?"

The first hunter says, " Funny you should ask, but we wuz just standing here a minute ago and a goat come a running out of them bushes doin' about a 'hunert miles an air and jumped headfirst into that thar hole!"

And the old farmer said, "Why that's impossible... I had him chained to an old transmission!"

GOAT

A little boy was overheard talking to himself as he strutted through the backyard, wearing his baseball cap and toting a ball and bat: "I'm the greatest hitter in the world," he announced. Then, he tossed the ball into the air, swung at it, and missed.

"Strike One!" he yelled. Undaunted, he picked up the ball and said again, "I'm the greatest hitter in the world!"

He tossed the ball into the air. When it came down he swung again and missed. "Strike Two!" he cried.

The boy then paused a moment to examine his bat and ball carefully. He spit on his hands and rubbed them together. He straightened his cap and said once more, "I'm the greatest hitter in the world!"

Again, he tossed the ball up in the air and swung at it. He missed. "Strike Three!"

"Wow!" he exclaimed. "I'm the greatest pitcher in the world!"

Golfer and Skydiver

What's the difference between a bad golfer and a bad skydiver?
A bad golfer first goes, WHACK! and THEN "Oh, no!"

Hunting Priorities

A group of Alabama friends went deer hunting and paired off in twos for the day. That night, one of the hunters returned alone, staggering under the weight of an eight-point buck.

"Where's Henry?" the others asked..

"Henry had a stroke of some kind. He's a couple of miles back up the trail," the unsuccessful hunter replied.

"You left Henry laying out there and carried the Deer back?" they inquired.

"A tough call," nodded the hunter. "But I figured no one is going to steal Henry!"

Perfect Eyesight

Arthur is 90 years old. He has played golf every day since his retirement 25 years ago. One day he arrives home looking downcast. "That's it," he tells his wife. "I'm giving up golf. My eyesight has gotten so bad that once I hit the ball, I couldn't see where it went."

His wife sympathizes and makes him a cup of tea. As they sit down she says, "Why don't you take my brother with you and give it one more try."

"That's no good" sighs Arthur, "your brother's a hundred and three. He can't help."

"He may be a hundred and three", says the wife, "but his eyesight is perfect."

So the next day Arthur heads off to the golf course with his brother-in-law.   He tees up, takes an almighty swing, and squints down the fairway.   He turns to the brother-in-law.   "Did you see the ball?"

"Of course I did!" replied the brother-in-law.   "I have perfect eyesight."

"Where did it go?" says Arthur.

"I don't remember."

Long ago when men cursed and beat the ground with sticks, it was called witchcraft.. Today, it's called golf...

Temperature Conversion Chart

The Official Canadian Temperature Conversion Chart

50° Fahrenheit (10° C) • Californians shiver uncontrollably. • Canadians plant gardens.

35° Fahrenheit (1.6° C) • Italian Cars won't start • Canadians drive with the windows down

32° Fahrenheit (0° C) • American water freezes • Canadian water gets thicker.

0° Fahrenheit (-17.9° C) • New York City landlords finally turn on the heat. • Canadians have the last cookout of the season.

-60° Fahrenheit (-51° C) • Santa Claus abandons the North Pole. • Canadian Girl Guides sell cookies door-to-door.

-109.9° Fahrenheit (-78.5° C) • Carbon dioxide freezes makes dry ice. • Canadians pull down their earflaps.

-173° Fahrenheit (-114° C) • Ethyl alcohol freezes. • Canadians get frustrated when they can't thaw the keg

-459.67° Fahrenheit (-273.15Â° C) • Absolute zero; all atomic motion stops. • Canadians start saying "cold, eh?"

-500° Fahrenheit (-295° C) • Hell freezes over. • The Toronto Maple Leafs win the Stanley Cup

That's Jack

A reporter was interviewing Jack Nicklaus. He said, "Jack, you are spectacular, your name is synonymous with the game of golf. You really know your way around the course. What is your secret?"

To which Jack replied, "The holes are numbered!"

The Laws of Golf

LAW 1: No matter how bad your last shot was, the worst is yet to come. This law does not expire on the 18th hole, since it has the supernatural tendency to extend over the course of a tournament, a summer and, eventually, a lifetime.

LAW 2: Your best round of golf will be followed almost immediately by your worst round ever. The probability of the latter increases with the number of people you tell about the former.

LAW 3: Brand new golf balls are water-magnetic. Though this cannot be proven in the lab, it is a known fact that the more expensive the golf ball, the greater its attraction to water.

LAW 4: Golf balls never bounce off of trees back into play. If one does, the tree is breaking a law of Nature and must be cut down.

LAW 5: No matter what causes a golfer to muff a shot, all his playing partners must solemnly chant "You looked up" or else invoke the Wrath of the Universe.

LAW 6: The higher a golfer's handicap, the more qualified he deems himself as an instructor.

LAW 7: Every par-three hole in the world has a secret desire to humiliate golfers. The shorter the hole, the greater its desire.

LAW 8: Topping a 3-iron is the most painful torture known to man.

LAW 9: Palm trees eat golf balls.

LAW 10: Sand is alive. If it isn't, how do you explain the way it works against you?

LAW 11: Golf carts always run out of power at the farthest point from the clubhouse.

LAW 12: A golfer hitting into your group will always be bigger than anyone in your group. Likewise, a group you accidentally hit into will consist of a football player, a professional wrestler, a convicted murderer and an IRS agent.

LAW 13: All 3-woods are demon-possessed.

LAW 14: Golf balls from the same sleeve tend to follow one another, particularly out of bounds or into the water (See Law 3).

LAW 15: A severe slice is a thing of awesome power and beauty.

LAW 16: "Nice lag" can usually be translated to "lousy putt." Similarly, "tough break" can usually be translated "way to miss an easy one, sucker."

LAW 17: The person you would most hate to lose to will always be the one who beats you.

LAW 18: The last three holes of a round will automatically adjust your score to what it really should be.

LAW 19: Golf should be given up at least twice per month.

LAW 20: All vows taken on a golf course shall be valid only until sunset.

World's Funniest Joke (as chosen in an internet poll)
Two hunters are out in the woods when one of them collapses. He doesn't seem to be breathing and his eyes are glazed. The other man pulls out his phone and calls emergency services. He gasps to the operator: "My friend is dead! What can I do?"
The operator in a calm, soothing voice replies: "Take it easy. I can help. First, let's make sure he's dead." There is a silence, then a shot is heard.
Back on the phone, the hunter says, "Ok, now what?"

Travel

Being Tactful

A bachelor kept a cat for companionship, and loved his cat more than life. He was planning a trip to England and entrusted the cat to his brother's care. As soon as he arrived in England he called his brother. "How is my cat?" he asked.

"Your cat is dead," came the reply.

"Oh my," he exclaimed. "Did you have to tell me that way?"

"How else can I tell you your cat's dead?" inquired the brother.

"You should have led me up to it gradually," said the bachelor. "For an example, when I called tonight you could have told me my cat was on the roof, but the Fire Department is getting it down. When I called tomorrow night, you could have told me that they dropped him and broke his back, but a fine surgeon is doing all he can for him. Then, when I called the third night, you could have told me the surgeon did all he could but my cat passed away. That way it wouldn't have been such a shock.

"By the way," he continued, "how's Mother?"

"Mother?" came the reply. "Oh, she's up on the roof, but the Fire Department is getting her down."

Best Wishes

Three guys, one smart, on average, and one a bit dim have begun a 40-mile hike home when they come upon a bush with an owl sitting atop it. To their surprise, the owl speaks,

"Weary travelers," he says, "I will give you each one wish."

The smart one says, "I want to be home and rich beyond my

dreams."

"Wish granted!" says the owl.

The average man says, "I want to be home and married to the most beautiful girl in the world."

"Wish granted!" says the owl.

The dim guy looks around and feels lonely. "I wish my friends were back," he says.

Customer Service

Angry customer: "Tell me, just what good is this stupid airline schedule, anyway?"

Agent: "It's simple, really. If it weren't for them, we'd have no way of knowing how late the planes are."

Generous Offer

A travel agent looked up from his desk to see an old lady and an old gentleman peering in the shop window at the posters showing the glamorous destinations around the world. The agent had had a good week and the dejected couple looking in the window gave him a rare feeling of generosity.

He called them into his shop: "I know that on your pension you could never hope to have a holiday, so I am sending you off to a fabulous resort at my expense, and I won't take no for an answer".

He took them inside and asked his secretary to write two flight tickets and book a room in a five- star hotel. They, as can be expected, gladly accepted, and were off!

About a month later the little old lady came in to his shop.

"And how did you like your holiday?" he asked eagerly.

"The flight was exciting and the room was lovely," she said. "I've come to thank you. But, one thing puzzled me. Who was that old guy I had to share the room with?"

Gripe Sheets

After every flight, pilots fill out a form called a gripe sheet, which conveys to the mechanics problems encountered with the aircraft during the flight that need repair or correction. Mechanics read and correct the problem, then respond in writing on the lower half of the form what remedial action was taken, and the pilot reviews the gripe sheets before the next flight. Here are some actual logged maintenance complaints and problems as submitted by Qantas pilots and the solution recorded by maintenance engineers. Qantas is the only major airline that has never had an accident.

(P = The problem logged by the pilot.)
(S = The solution and action taken by the engineers.)

P: Left inside main tire almost needs replacement.
S: Almost replaced left inside main tire.

P: Test flight OK, except auto-land very rough.
S: Auto-land not installed on this aircraft.

P: Something loose in cockpit.
S: Something tightened in cockpit.

P: Dead bugs on windshield.
S: Live bugs on backorder.

P: Autopilot in altitude-hold mode produces a 200 feet per minute descent.
S: Cannot reproduce problem on ground.

P: Evidence of leak on right main landing gear.
S: Evidence removed.

P: DME volume unbelievably loud.
S: DME volume set to more believable level.

P: Friction locks cause throttle levers to stick.
S: That's what they're there for.

P: IFF inoperative.
S: IFF always inoperative in OFF mode.

P: Suspected crack in windshield.
S: Suspect you're right.

P: Number 3 engine missing.
S: Engine found on right wing after brief search.

P: Aircraft handles funny.
S: Aircraft warned to straighten up, fly right, and be serious.

P: Target radar hums.
S: Reprogrammed target radar with lyrics.

P: Mouse in cockpit.
S: Cat installed.

P: Noise coming from under instrument panel. Sounds like a midget pounding on something with a hammer.
S: Took hammer away from midget.

Mix up

After stopping for drinks at an illegal bar, a Zimbabwean bus driver found that the 20 mental patients he was supposed to be transporting from Harare to Bulawayo had escaped...

Not wanting to admit his incompetence, the driver went to a nearby bus stop and offered everyone waiting there a free ride. He then delivered the passengers to the
mental hospital, telling the staff that the patients were very excitable and prone to bizarre fantasies.

The deception wasn't discovered for 3 days.

Nine Months Later

Jack decided to go skiing with his buddy, Bob. They loaded up in Jack's mini-van and headed north. After driving for a few hours, they got caught in a terrible blizzard. They pulled into a nearby farm and asked the attractive lady who answered the door if they could spend the night.

"I realize it's a terrible weather out there and I have the huge house all to myself, but I'm recently widowed," she explained. "I'm afraid the neighbors will talk if I let you stay in my house."

"Don't worry," Jack said. "We'll be happy to sleep in the barn. And if the weather breaks, we'll be gone at first light."

The lady agreed, and the two men found their way to the barn and settled in for the night. Come morning, the weather had cleared, and they got on their way. They enjoyed a great weekend of skiing.

About nine months later, Jack got an unexpected letter from an attorney. It took him a few minutes to figure it out, but he finally determined that it was from the attorney of that attractive widow he had met on the ski weekend.

He dropped in on his friend Bob and asked, "Bob, do you remember that good-looking widow from the farm we stayed at on our ski holiday up north?"

"Yes, I do."

"Did you happen to get up in the middle of the night, go up to the house and pay her a visit?"

"Yes," Bob said, a little embarrassed about being found out. "I have to admit, I did."

"And did you happen to use my name instead of telling her your name?"

Bob's face turned red and he said, "Yeah, sorry Buddy, I'm afraid I did. Why do you ask?"

"She just died and left me everything."

The Bus Conductor

A little old lady is on a bus, buying a ticket from the bus conductor. She fumbles in a voluminous bag for the correct change. After 15 minutes the conductor becomes so enraged that he hits her on the head with the ticket-dispenser, and the poor old dear dies instantly. Not surprisingly, he is convicted and put on death row. Just before he is to be electrocuted, his last request is for 12 pounds of bananas, which he devours. They strap him into the chair, flip the switch, and nothing happens! He just sits there, smiling. According to tradition, this is considered a reprieve from God, so the man is freed.

Somehow, he gets his old job back, and he happily dispenses tickets until he sees a girl stick her wad of gum onto a seat on the bus. Enraged, he lunges out with the ticket dispenser, breaking the offender's neck and killing her.

Again, he is convicted and sent to death row. He again eats the 12 pounds of bananas and, lo and behold, the electricity doesn't harm him. So again, he is set free.

Amazingly, he regains his job! It takes him just one day to lose his temper and beat to death a young boy who is chewing on his bus ticket. He returns to death row.

Again he eats 12 pound of bananas before the execution. This time the executioner cleans the contacts, makes him sit in a bucket of water, he tries everything - but the conductor survives the electrocution with nary a twitch.

At this point, the executioner can take no more – his professional pride has been hurt. Before setting our friend free again, he asks him his secret - what is it with the bananas?

"Oh, the bananas have nothing to do with it," replies our friend. "I'm just a really bad conductor."

Watch the Signs

What happened?" asked the hospital visitor to the heavily bandaged man sitting up in bed.

"Well, I went down to Margate at the weekend and decided to take a ride on the roller coaster. As we came up to the top of the highest loop, I noticed a little sign by the side of the track. I tried to read it but it was very small and I couldn't make it out. I was so curious that I decided to go round again, but we went by so quickly that I couldn't see what the sign said.

By now, I was determined to read that sign so I went round a third time. As we reached the top, I stood up in the car to get a better view."

"And did you manage to see what the sign said this time?" asked the visitor.

"Yes."

"What did it say?"

"Don't stand up in the car!"

Why'd They Do That?

Historic Windsor Castle, outside of London, is directly in the flight path of Heathrow International Airport.

While a group of tourists was standing outside the castle admiring the elegant structure, a plane flew overhead at a relatively low altitude, making a tremendous noise.

One particularly annoyed tourist whined, "Why did they build the castle so close to the airport?"

Yes Dear

Late one afternoon, the Air Force guys out at Area 51 are surprised to see a Cessna landing at their "secret" base. They immediately impound the aircraft and haul the pilot into an interrogation room.

The pilot's story is that he took off out of Las Vegas, got lost and found the base just as he was about to run out of fuel. The Air Force starts a full security check on the guy and hold him overnight. The next day they are finally convinced that the guy really was lost and is not a spy. They gas up his airplane, give him a terrifying "you did not see a base" briefing complete with threats of spending the rest of his life in prison. They say Vegas is that-a-way on this heading and send him off.

The next day, here comes the Cessna again. Once again the MPs surround the plane, only this time there are two people in the plane.

The same pilot jumps out and says: "Do anything you want to me, but my wife is in the plane and you have to tell her where I was last night....."

Points to Ponder

"The church speaks of things that are real as though they are not; the theatre speaks of things that are not real as though they are." - Charles Garrick (19th Century actor)

"God wants spiritual fruit, not religious nuts."

"God loves us enough to accept us as we are. But He loves us too much to leave us that way."- G. Robert Jacks

"In the beginning the church was a fellowship of men and women centered on the living Christ. Then the church moved to Greece, where it became a philosophy. Then it moved to Rome, where it became an institution. Next, it moved to Europe, where it became a culture. And, finally, it moved to America, where it became an enterprise." Richard C. Halverson

"When you get tangled up in your problems, be still. God wants you to be still so He can untangle the knot."

"It's all right to sit on your pity pot every now and again. Just remember to flush it occasionally!"

"Preach to broken hearts and you will never lack a congregation because there is a broken heart in every pew." Joseph Parker

"Most middle- class Americans tend to worship their work, work at their play, and play at their worship. As a result, their meanings and values are distorted, their relationships disintegrate faster than they can keep them in repair and their lifestyles resemble a cast of characters in search of a plot." Gordon Dahl

"The job of a football coach is to make men do what they don't want to do, in order to be what they've always wanted to be."- Tom Landry

"Do the math ... count your blessings."

"The most important things in your home are the people."

Old legal adage: "When the law is not on your side you argue the facts, when the facts are not on your side you argue the law, but when neither the law nor facts are on your side – you pound the table."

"All models are wrong, but some are useful". George Box

"Those who feel entitled to everything are seldom thankful for anything." Bobby Huguley

"In matters of style, swim with the current; in matters of principle, stand like a rock."   Thomas Jefferson

"If a leader can't get a message across clearly and motivate others to act on it, then having a message doesn't even matter." Gilbert Amelio

"Beauty is only skin deep, but ugly goes clean to the bone" Dorothy Parker

"You will find as you look back upon your life that the moments when you have really lived are the moments when you have done things in a spirit of love." Henry Drummond

"Criticism has the power to do good when there is something that must be destroyed, dissolved or reduced, but it is capable only of harm when there is something to be built." Carl Jung

"Insults should be written in the sand, and praises carved in stone. Arab Proverb

"Yesterday is gone. Tomorrow has not yet come. We have only today. Let us begin." Mother Teresa

"The greater the obstacle, the more glory in overcoming it." – Moliere

"I have not failed. I've just found 10,000 ways that won't work."

— Thomas A. Edison

"People are lonely because they build walls instead of bridges."
Anonymous

"Nothing is real to you until you experience it, otherwise it's just hearsay."

"There are two kinds of people in the world, those who get it and those who don't. The vast majority are in the second category- they just don't have a clue. We see ourselves in the first category. It's hard to put up with those in the second category and with those who put us in that category." Bobby Huguley

"If you're going to burn your bridges, you'd better be a darn good swimmer." Lou Holtz

"In times of profound change, the learners inherit the earth, while the learned find themselves beautifully equipped to deal with a world that no longer exists." Eric Hoffer

"Nobody can go back and start a new beginning, but anyone can start today and make a new ending." Maria Robinson

"The most important thing in the Olympic Games is not to win but to take part, just as the most important thing in life is not the triumph, but the struggle. The essential thing is not to have conquered, but to have fought well." The Olympic Creed

"Winning isn't getting ahead of others, it is getting ahead of yourself." Roger Staubach

"Frugality is one of the most beautiful and joyful words in the English language, and yet one that we are culturally cut off from understanding and enjoying. The consumption society has made us feel that happiness lies in having things, and has failed to teach us the happiness of not having things." Elise Boulding

"You know you've achieved perfection in design, not when you have nothing more to add, but when you have nothing more to take away." Antoine-Marie-Roger de Saint-Exupery

"Blessed is the man who, having nothing to say, abstains from giving evidence of the fact." George Eliot

"The real art of conversation is not only to say the right thing at the right place but to leave unsaid the wrong thing at the tempting moment." Dorothy Nevill

"Most conversations are simply monologues delivered in the presence of witnesses."

"The two words 'information' and 'communication' are often used interchangeably, but they signify quite different things. Information is giving out; communication is getting through." Sydney J. Harris

"Silence is often misinterpreted, but never misquoted."

"Every child is an artist. The problem is how to remain an artist once he grows up." Pablo Picasso

"You gain strength, courage, and confidence by every experience in which you stop to look fear in the face. You are able to say to yourself, `I lived through this horror. I can take the next thing that comes along.' The danger lies in refusing to face the fear, in not daring to come to grips with it." Eleanor Roosevelt

"It's a little like wrestling a gorilla. You don't quit when you're tired. You quit when the gorilla is tired." Robert Strauss

"The greatest oak was once a little nut who held its ground." Author Unknown

"Education is not the filling of a pail, but the lighting of a fire." William Butler Yeats

"Never tell people how to do things. Tell them what to do and they will surprise you with their ingenuity." General George Smith Patton, Jr.

"The beauty of empowering others is that your own power is not diminished in the process." Barbara Colorose

"A good leader inspires people to have confidence in the leader; a great leader inspires people to have confidence in themselves." Eleanor Roosevelt

"Flatter me, and I may not believe you. Criticize me, and I may not like you. Ignore me, and I may not forgive you. Encourage me, and I will not forget you." William Arthur Ward

"When I was a child, my mother said to me: If you become a soldier, you'll be a general. If you become a monk you'll end up as the Pope. Instead I became a painter and wound up as Picasso."- Pablo Picasso

"The only man who behaves sensibly is my tailor; he takes my measurements anew every time he sees me, while all the rest go on with their old measurements and expect me to fit them." George Bernard Shaw

"The most serious mistakes are not being made as a result of wrong answers. The truly dangerous thing is asking the wrong question." Peter Drucker

"One of the great mistakes is to judge policies and programs by their intentions rather than their results" Milton Friedman

"Excellence is to do a common thing in an uncommon way." Booker T. Washington

"He who knows not, and knows not that he knows not, is a fool, shun him;

He who knows not, and knows that he knows not, is a child, teach him.

He who knows, and knows not that he knows, is asleep, wake him.

He who knows, and knows that he knows, is wise, follow him." Proverb

"Forgiveness does not change the past, but it does enlarge the future." Paul Boese

"To forgive is to set a prisoner free and discover that the prisoner was you." Lewis B. Smedes

"Unforgiveness is like drinking poison and hoping the other person will die."" Unknown

"A grudge is a heavy thing to carry."

"Your big opportunity may be right where you are now." Napoleon Hill

"If we all worked on the assumption that what is accepted as true were really true, there would be little hope of advance." Orville Wright

"What we do for ourselves dies with us. What we do for others and the world remains and is immortal." Albert Pike

"Feeling gratitude and not expressing it is like wrapping a present and not giving it." William Arthur Ward

"None are so empty as those who are full of themselves." Benjamin Whichcot

"The way to get good ideas is to get lots of ideas, and throw the bad ones away." Dr. Linus Pauling

"Talent is God given. Be humble.
Fame is man-given. Be grateful.
Conceit is self-given. Be careful." John Wooden

It's easy to come up with new ideas; the hard part is letting go of what worked for you two years ago, but will soon be out of date." Roger von Oech

"No one can make you feel inferior without your consent." Eleanor Roosevelt

"We judge others by their behavior. We judge ourselves by our intentions." Henry Wadsworth Longfellow

"Don't judge each day by the harvest you reap, but by the seeds you plant." Robert Louis Stevenson

"Too many people spend money they haven't earned, to buy things they don't want, to impress people they don't like." Will Rogers

"It is impossible for a man to learn what he thinks he already knows." Epicetus

"It's not the will to win that matters—everyone has that. It's the will to prepare to win that matters." Paul "Bear" Bryant

"Many of life's failures are people who did not realize how close they were to success when they gave up." Thomas Edison

"Live as if you were to die tomorrow. Learn as if you were to live forever." attributed to Mahatma Gandhi

"The man who complains about the way the ball bounces is likely to be the one who dropped it." Lou Holtz

"It is more important to know where you are going than to get there quickly. Do not mistake activity for achievement." Mabel Newcomber

"There is never enough time to do everything, but there is always enough time to do the most important thing." Brian Tracy

"It's what you learn after you know it all that counts." John

Wooden
        "Anyone who stops learning is old, whether at twenty or eighty. Anyone who keeps learning stays young. The greatest thing in life is to keep your mind young." Henry Ford

        "Growing old is inevitable, growing UP is optional."

        "He who dies with the most toys is still dead."

        "Time is what we want most, but what we use worst." William Penn

        "Sticks in a bundle are unbreakable." African proverb

        Hoffer's law: When people are free to do what they want they usually imitate one another.

        "Honest criticism is hard to take, particularly from a relative, a friend, an acquaintance, or a stranger." Franklin P. Jones

        "Hope is the ability to hear the music of the future.
        Faith is having the courage to dance to it today."

        "Hospital is a place where they wake you up to give you a sleeping pill."

"Hospitality is making your guests feel at home -- even when you wish they were."

"A critic is to art what a pigeon is to a statue." George Bernard Shaw

"People who cannot find time for recreation are obliged sooner or later to find time for illness." John Wanamaker

"Laugh every day, it's like inner jogging."

"There is no key to happiness. The door is always open."

"The great composer does not set to work because he is inspired, but becomes inspired because he is working. Beethoven, Wagner, Bach and Mozart settled down day after day to the job in hand with as much regularity as an accountant settles down each day to his figures. They didn't waste time waiting for inspiration." Earnest Newman

"If you worry, you didn't pray. If you pray, don't worry."

"As a child of God, prayer is kind of like calling home every day."

"No matter how big and tough a problem may be, get rid of confusion by taking one little step toward solution. Do something. Then try again. At the worst so long as you don't do it the same way twice, you will eventually use up all the wrong ways of doing it and thus the next try will be the right one." George F. Nordenhol

"Before it can be solved, a problem must be clearly stated and defined." William Feather

"Dear God, I have a problem -- it's me."

"The most important thing to do in solving a problem is to begin." Frank Tyger

"A man who wants to lead the orchestra must turn his back on the crowd." James Crook

"When a man does not know what harbor he is making for, no wind is the right wind." Seneca

"He who trims himself to suit everyone will soon whittle himself away." Raymond Hull

"You were born an original. Don't die a copy." John Mason

"We Cannot do everything at once but we can do something at once." Calvin Coolidge

"Well done is better than well said." Benjamin Franklin

"The time is always right to do what is right."- Martin Luther King Jr.

"Most people want to serve God, but only in an advisory position."

"One reason God created time was so there would be a place to bury the failures of the past." James Long

"Humility is not thinking less of yourself, it's thinking of yourself less." C.S. Lewis

"Let me write the songs of a nation: I don't care who writes its laws." Scottish politician Andrew Fletcher 1653-1716

"Faith is the ability to not panic."

"I've missed more than 9,000 shots in my career. I've lost almost 300 games. 26 times, I've been trusted to take the game winning shot and missed. I've failed over and over and over again in my life. And that is why I succeed." – Michael Jordan

"You have to expect things of yourself before you can do them." — Michael Jordan

*"In a crisis, don't hide behind anything or anybody. They're going to find you anyway."-
Paul "Bear" Bryant

"Excellence is the gradual result of always striving to do better."
- Pat Riley

"The quality of a person's life is in direct proportion to their commitment to excellence, regardless of their chosen field of endeavor." - Vince Lombardi

"Blessed are the flexible for they shall not be bent out of shape."

"[What matters most] is not the honor that you take with you, but the heritage you leave behind." - Branch Rickey

"Momentum is the most unstoppable force in sports. The only way to stop it is if you get in your own way, start making stupid mistakes or stop believing in yourself."
~ Rocco Mediate

"A lifetime of training for just ten seconds." - Jesse Owens (on running the 100-meter dash in the Olympics)

"I run on the road long before I dance under the lights." - Muhammad Ali

"It's better to look ahead and prepare than to look back and regret." - Jackie Joyner-Kersee

"I am a member of a team, and I rely on the team, I defer to it and sacrifice for it, because the team, not the individual, is the ultimate champion."
~ Mia Hamm

"We do not remember days, but moments."

"Life is moving too fast, so enjoy your precious moments."

"Success is peace of mind which is a direct result of self-satisfaction in knowing you made the effort to become the best that you are capable of becoming." - John Wooden

"In order to have a winner, the team must have a feeling of unity. Every player must put the team first, ahead of personal glory." - Paul "Bear" Bryant

"It's easy to get good players. Getting them to play together, that's the hard part." - Casey Stengel

"He who angers you controls you!"

"It's not whether you get knocked down; it's whether you get back up that counts." - Vince Lombardi

Inspirational Quotes
with Scripture

"Music washes away from the soul the dust of everyday life." - Red Auerbach

"The Lord is my strength and my song; He has become my salvation. He is my God, and I will praise Him, my father's God, and I will exalt Him." Exodus 15:2

"If you please God it doesn't matter who you displease, but if you displease God it doesn't matter who you please." - Vance Havner

"You must obey my laws and be careful to follow my decrees. I am the LORD your God." Leviticus 18:4.

"There is a God we want, and there is a God who is. These are not the same God. The turning point of our lives is when we stop seeking the God we want and start seeking the God who is." - Patrick Morley

"... seek the LORD your God, you will find him if you look for him with all your heart and with all your soul." Deuteronomy 4:29

"He who stands uprightly does not have a crooked shadow." - Chinese Proverb

"Walk in all the way that the LORD your God has commanded you, so that you may live and prosper and prolong your days in the land that you will possess." Deuteronomy 5:33

"As a follower of Christ we aren't always sure where we're going, but we are sure who we're following."   Dietrich Bonhoffer-

"It is the LORD your God you must follow, and him you must revere. Keep his commands and obey him; serve him and hold fast to him." Deuteronomy 13:4

"Courage is doing what you're afraid to do. There can be no courage unless you're scared." - Eddie Rickenbacker

"Be strong and courageous. Do not be afraid or terrified because of them, for the LORD your God goes with you; he will never leave you nor forsake you." Deuteronomy 31:6

"Hold yourself responsible for a higher standard than anybody else expects of you." - Henry Ward Beecher

"...do not turn from it to the right or to the left, that you may be successful wherever you go." Joshua 1:7b)

"Without courage all other virtues lose their meaning." - Winston Churchill

"Have I not commanded you? Be strong and courageous. Do not be terrified; do not be discouraged, for the LORD your God will be with you wherever you go." Joshua 1:9

"And the day came...when the risk it took to remain tight in the bud... became greater than the risk it took to blossom." Anonymous

"Consecrate yourselves, for tomorrow, the Lord will do amazing things among you." Joshua 3:5

"The choice you make today will usually affect tomorrow."

"...then choose for yourselves this day whom you will serve, whether the gods your forefathers served beyond the River, or the gods of the Amorites, in whose land you are living. But as for me and my household, we will serve the LORD."   Joshua 24:15

"You have to expect things of yourself before you can do them."— Michael Jordan

"Be strong; show what you're made of! Do what God tells you. Walk in the paths he shows you: Follow the life-map absolutely, keep an eye out for the signposts, his course for life set out in the revelation to Moses; then you'll get on well in whatever you do and wherever you go." -1 Kings 2:2-3 (The Message)

"Holy Shoddy is still shoddy!" - Elton Trueblood

"I will not offer God that which costs me nothing." -King David, a man after God's own heart" - 1 Chronicles 21:24

"What we do not see, what most of us never suspect of existing, is the silent but irresistible power which comes to the rescue of those who fight on in the face of discouragement." - Napoleon Hill

"... "Be strong and courageous, and do the work. Do not be afraid or discouraged, for the LORD God, my God, is with you. He will not fail you or forsake you..." 1 Chronicles 28:20

"Worship involves a humbling but delightful sense of admiring awe and astonished wonder. It is delightful to worship God, but it is also a humbling thing; and the man who has not been humbled in the presence of God will never be a worshiper of God at all. He may be a church member who keeps the rules and obeys the discipline, and who tithes and goes to conferences, but he'll never be a worshiper unless he is deeply humbled." - A.W. Tozer

"If my people, who are called by my name, will humble themselves and pray and seek my face and turn from their wicked ways, then will I hear from heaven and will forgive their sin and will heal their land."   -II Chronicles 7:14

"Since God has given me a cheerful heart, He will forgive me for serving Him cheerfully." - Franz Joseph Haydn

"Do not be grieved. The joy of the Lord is your strength!" - Nehemiah 8:10

"The happiest people don't necessarily have the best of everything. They just make the best of everything."

"Blessed is the man who does not walk in the counsel of the wicked or stand in the way of sinners or sit in the seat of mockers. But his delight is in the law of the LORD, and on his law he meditates day and night. He is like a tree planted by streams of water, which yields its fruit in season and whose leaf does not wither. Whatever he does prospers." Psalm 1:1-3

"The real voyage of discovery consists of not in seeking new landscapes but in having new eyes." ~ Marcel Proust

"The precepts of the LORD are right, giving joy to the heart. The commands of the LORD are radiant, giving light to the eyes." Psalm 19:8

"Most of the important things in the world have been accomplished by people who have kept on trying when there seemed to be no hope at all." - *Dale Carnegie*

"Be strong and take heart, all you who hope in the LORD." Psalm 31:24

"A bird doesn't sing because it has an answer, it sings because it has a song!" -Joan Augland

"Rejoice in the LORD and be glad, you righteous; sing, all you who are upright in heart!" Psalm 32:11

"The glory of God is a human being fully alive!"   St. Irenaeus

"Delight yourself in the LORD and he will give you the desires of your heart." Psalm 37:4

"Music is God's gift to man, the only art of Heaven given to earth, the only art of earth we take to Heaven." -Walter Savage Landor

"He put a new song in my mouth, a hymn of praise to our God. Many will see and fear and put their trust in the LORD." Psalm 40:3

"Stop telling God how big your storm is. Instead tell your storm how big your GOD is." Cindy Hockenjos

"Never be afraid to trust an unknown future to a known God."- Corrie Ten Boom

"God is our refuge and strength, an ever-present help in trouble. Therefore we will not fear..."   Psalm 46:1-2a

"People are like stained-glass windows. They sparkle and shine when the sun is out, but when the darkness sets in, their true beauty is revealed only if there is a light from within." (Elizabeth Kübler-Ross)

"Create in me a clean heart, God" (Psalm 51:10)

"Life is a grindstone. Whether it grinds you down or polishes you up depends upon what you are made of." - John C. Maxwell

"Cast your cares on the LORD and he will sustain you; he will never let the righteous fall." Psalm 55:22

"We don't stop playing because we grow old... we grow old because we stop playing."

"Shout with joy to God, all the earth! Sing the glory of his name; make his praise glorious!" Psalm 66:1-2

"What we see depends mainly on what we look for." - John Lubbock

"Come and see what God has done, how awesome his works in man's behalf!" Psalm 66:5

"Where does the idea come from that if what we are doing is fun, it can't be God's will? The God who made giraffes, has a sense of humor. Make no mistake about that." -Catherine Marshall

Our mouths were filled with laughter, our tongues with songs of joy. Then it was said among the nations, "The LORD has done great things for them." Psalm 126:2

"Learn carefully from the mistakes of others. There isn't enough time for you to make all of them yourself.

"For the Lord gives wisdom: out of His mouth comes knowledge and understanding." Proverbs 2:6

"When a man does not know what harbor he is making for, no wind is the right wind."   - Seneca

"Trust in the LORD with all your heart and lean not on your own understanding; in all your ways acknowledge him, and he will make your paths straight. Proverbs 3:5-6

"No one keeps up his enthusiasm automatically. Enthusiasm must be nourished with new actions, new aspirations, new efforts, new vision. It is one''s own fault if his enthusiasm is gone; he has failed to feed it." -Papyrus

A wise man has great power, and a man of knowledge

increases strength; (Proverbs 24:5)

"Many people will walk in and out of your life, but only true friends leave footprints in your heart." Eleanor Roosevelt

"The heartfelt counsel of a friend is as sweet as perfume and incense" Proverbs 27:9

Some Powerful words:
1. The most bitter word is **alone**.
2. The most tragic word is **death**.
3. The most beautiful word is **love.**
4. The most cruel word is **revenge**.
5. The most peaceful word is **tranquil.**
6. The saddest word is **forgotten.**
7. The warmest word is **friendship.**
8. The coldest word is **no.**
9. The most comforting word is **faith.**
10. The most reverent word is **mother.**

"Charm is deceptive, and beauty is fleeting; but a woman who fears the LORD is to be praised. Give her the reward she has earned, and let her works bring her praise at the city gate." Proverbs 31:30-31

"The greatest possession you have is the 24 hours directly ahead of you." (Unknown)

"For there is a time for every purpose and for every work." Ecclesiastics 3:17b

"Those who feel entitled to everything are seldom thankful for anything."

"Moreover, when God gives any man wealth and possessions, and enables him to enjoy them, to accept his lot and be happy in his work--this is a gift of God." Ecclesiastes 5:19

"The place to be happy is...where you are. The time to be happy is...now. The way to be happy is...to make others happy." (Roger Ingersoll)

"When times are good, be happy; but when times are bad, consider: God has made the one as well as the other." (Ecclesiastics 7:14)

We cannot do everything at once, but we can do something at once" – Calvin Coolidge

"Whatever your hand finds to do, do it with all your might, for in the grave, where you are going, there is neither working nor planning nor knowledge nor wisdom." Eccl 9:10

"After silence, that which is nearest to expressing the inexpressible is...music." Huxley

"O Lord, You are my God; I will exalt You and praise Your name...for in perfect faithfulness, You have done marvelous things

planned long ago." Isaiah 25:1 (NIV)

"There is an eagle in me that wants to soar, and there is a hippopotamus in me that wants to wallow in the mud." – Carl Sandburg

"but those who hope in the LORD will renew their strength. They will soar on wings like eagles; they will run and not grow weary, they will walk and not be faint." Isaiah 40:31

"Unless you believe the gospel, everything you do will be driven by either pride or fear." Tim Keller

So do not fear, for I am with you; do not be dismayed, for I am your God. I will strengthen you and help you; I will uphold you with my righteous right hand. Isaiah 41:10

"We are what we imagine. The greatest tragedy that can befall one is to go through life unimagined." -Scott Momaday

"Forget the former things! Do not dwell on the past. See, I am doing a new thing!"" Isaiah 43:18-19a

"The best thing about the future is that it comes only one day at a time."- Abraham Lincoln

"For I know the plans I have for you," declares the LORD, "plans to prosper you and not to harm you, plans to give you hope and a future. Then you will call upon me and come and pray to me, and I

will listen to you." Jeremiah 29:11 -12

"People are like stained-glass windows. They sparkle and shine when the sun is out, but when the darkness sets in their true beauty is revealed only if there is light from within."
— Elisabeth Kübler-Ross

"…let your light shine before men, that they may see your good deeds and praise your Father in heaven." Matthew 5:16

"If you try to be everything to everybody, you will end up being nothing to anybody."   - Vance Havner

"Not everything that can be counted counts, and not everything that counts can be counted."

But seek first his kingdom and his righteousness, and all these things will be given to you as well. Matthew 6:33

"You can't change the past, but you can ruin the present by worrying over the future."

Therefore, do not worry about tomorrow, for tomorrow will worry about itself. Each day has enough trouble of its own." Matthew 6:34

"Before you criticize a man, walk a mile in his shoes. That way, when you do criticize him, you'll be a mile away and have his shoes." Steve Martin

"Do not judge, or you too will be judged. For in the same way you judge others, you will be judged, and with the measure you use, it will be measured to you." Matthew 7:1-2

"People who cannot find time for recreation are obliged sooner or later to find time for illness." - John Wanamaker

"Come to me, all you who are weary and burdened, and I will give you rest." – Jesus   (Matthew 11:28)

"Education is not the filling of a pail, but the lighting of a fire." William Butler Yeats

"Take my yoke upon you and learn from me, for I am gentle and humble in heart, and you will find rest for your souls." Matthew 11:29

C.S. Lewis: ".... the church exists for nothing else but to draw men into Christ, to make them little Christs. If they are not doing that, all the cathedrals, clergy, missions, sermons, even the Bible itself, are simply a waste of time." - from *Mere Christianity*

Jesus Christ:... "If anyone would come after me, he must deny himself and take up his cross and follow me. For whoever wants to save his life will lose it, but whoever loses his life for me will find it. What good will it be for a man if he gains the whole world, yet forfeits his soul? Or what can a man give in exchange for his soul? Matthew 16:24-26

"If Christ is risen, nothing else matters. And if Christ is not risen -- nothing else matters." Jaroslav Pelikan

"He is not here; he has risen, just as he said. Come and see the place where he lay"- Matthew 28:6

"Human beings can alter their lives by altering their attitudes of mind." – William James

Love the Lord your God with all your heart and with all your soul and with all your mind and with all your strength.' Mark 12:30

"In this world it is not what we take up, but what we give up, that makes us rich." - Henry Ward Beecher

"Do to others as you would have them do to you." Jesus (Luke 6:31)

There are two kinds of people: those who say to God, "Thy will be done," and those to whom God says, "All right, then, have it your way." C. S. Lewis

Then he said to them all: "If anyone would come after me, he must deny himself and take up his cross daily and follow me. For whoever wants to save his life will lose it, but whoever loses his life for me will save it. Luke 9:23-24

"God is in the details."

"Consider how the lilies grow. They do not labor or spin. Yet I tell you, not even Solomon in all his splendor was dressed like one of these. If that is how God clothes the grass of the field, which is here today, and tomorrow is thrown into the fire, how much more will he clothe you, O you of little faith!" Luke 12:27-28

"If we are going to worship in Spirit, we must develop a spirit of worship." Michael Catt

**"Yet a time is coming and has now come when the true worshipers will worship the Father in spirit and truth, for they are the kind of worshipers the Father seeks.
God is spirit, and his worshipers must worship in spirit and in truth." John 4:23-24**

"The great tragedy of life is not death -- but that which dies inside us while we live."   - Norman Cousins

"I came so they can have real and eternal life, more and better life than they ever dreamed of." - Jesus (John 10:10 *The Message*)

"Action seems to follow feeling, but really action and feeling go together; and by regulating the action, which is under the more direct control of the will, we can indirectly regulate the feeling, which is not." William James

"A new command I give you: Love one another. As I have loved you, so you must love one another. By this all men will know that you are my disciples, if you love one another." – Jesus (John 13:34-35)

"Selfless love is always costly; fear can't afford it pride doesn't understand it and friends never forget it." Bob Goff

"Greater love has no one than this: to lay down one's life for one's friends." John 15:13

"If I find in myself a desire which no experience in this world can satisfy, the most probable explanation is that I was made for another world." C.S. Lewis

Jesus said, "My kingdom is not of this world. If it were, my servants would fight to prevent my arrest by the Jews. But now my kingdom is from another place." John 18:36

"In the last analysis, what we are communicates far more eloquently than anything we say or do." - Stephen Covey

"Keep watch over yourselves and all the flock of which the Holy Spirit has made you overseers. Be shepherds of the church of God, which he bought with his own blood." Acts 20: 28

God proved his love on the cross. When Christ hung and bled, it was God saying to the world, "I love you." --Billy Graham

"But God demonstrates his own love for us in this: While we were still sinners, Christ died for us." Romans 5:8

"Act as if it were impossible to fail."   - Dorothea Brande

"... If God is for us, who can be against us?   Romans 8:31

"The Bible tells us to love our neighbors, and also to love our enemies, probably because they are generally the same people."

"Love from the center of who you are; don't fake it. Run for dear life from evil; hold on for dear life to good. Be good friends who love deeply; practice playing second fiddle." Romans 12:9-10 *The Message*

"The most useful person in the world today is the man or woman who knows how to get along with other people. Human relations is the most important science in living."
- Stanley C. Allyn

"Let no debt remain outstanding, except the continuing debt to love one another, for he who loves his fellowman has fulfilled the law". Romans 13:8

"The more I think it over the more I feel that there is nothing more truly artistic than to love people." - Vincent Van Gogh

"Love your neighbor as yourself." – Jesus

Wherever a human being exists, there is an opportunity to do a kindness. —Seneca

"So let's agree to use all our energy in getting along with each other. Help others with encouraging words; don't drag them down by finding fault." -Romans 14:19 (*The Message*)

"There is just one way to bring up a child in the way he should go and that is to travel that way yourself." - Abraham Lincoln

"Do not cause anyone to stumble, whether Jews, Greeks or the church of God." 1 Corinthians 10:32

"The art of being wise is the art of knowing what to overlook." William James

Love is patient, love is kind. It does not envy, it does not boast, it is not proud. It is not rude, it is not self-seeking, it is not easily angered, it keeps no record of wrongs. 1 Corinthians 13:4-5

"Before you are a leader, success is all about growing yourself. When you become a leader, success is all about growing others." - Jack Welch

"Again, if the trumpet does not sound a clear call, who will get ready for battle?" 1 Corinthians 14:8

"There are many voices vying for attention today. And some of these voices can sound so good – present their story so effectively – be packaged so incredibly – yet, be so far from the message of the Master. May we constantly pray with a pure heart, good conscience and sincere faith for the discernment that only God can provide. May we consistently listen, with perfect pitch, to the Voice of Truth." Randy Vader

"For who has known the mind of the Lord that he may instruct Him?" But we have the mind of Christ. 1 Corinthians 2:16

"The Day you were born, the world rejoiced- and you cried. Live in such a manner that when you die, the world will cry – and you will rejoice." (Indian Proverb)

Therefore, if any man be in Christ, he is a new creature: old things are passed away; behold, all things are become new. 2 Corinthians 5:16-18

Are you growing as A Christian? Are you more Christlike than you were last week, last month, last year...?

"Be diligent in these matters; give yourself wholly to them, so that everyone may see your progress. Watch your life and doctrine closely. Persevere in them, because if you do, you will save both yourself and your hearers." 1 Timothy 4:15-16

"Good and evil both increase at compound interest." -C.S. Lewis

"Do not be deceived: God cannot be mocked. A man reaps what he sows. The one who sows to please his sinful nature, from that nature will reap destruction; the one who sows to please the Spirit, from the Spirit will reap eternal life." Galatians 6:7-8

"It's not whether you get knocked down; it's whether you get back up that counts." - Vince Lombardi

"Let us not become weary in doing good, for at the proper time we will reap a harvest if we do not give up." Galatians 6:9

"Maintaining a complicated life...is a great way to avoid changing it." Elaine St. James

"I urge you...to live a life worthy of the calling you have received. Be completely humble and gentle...be patient...bearing with one another in love. Make every effort to keep the unity of the spirit through the bond of peace." Ephesians 4:1-3

"No man is an island, entire of itself; every man is a piece of the continent." — John Donne

"Remember upon the conduct of each depends the fate of all." — Alexander the Great

"Sticks in a bundle are unbreakable"— Kenyan Proverb

"Be completely humble and gentle; be patient, bearing with one another in love. Make every effort to keep the unity of the Spirit through the bond of peace." Ephesians 4:2-3

"Could we change our attitude, we should not only see life differently, but life itself would come to be different. Life would undergo a change of appearance because we ourselves had undergone a change of attitude." Katherine Mansfield

"You were taught, with regard to your former way of life, to put off your old self, which is being corrupted by its deceitful desires; to be made new in the attitude of your minds;" Ephesians 4:22 -23

"Kind words can be short and easy to speak, but their echoes are truly endless." – Mother Teresa

"Speak to one another with psalms, hymns and spiritual songs. Sing and make music in your heart to the Lord, always giving thanks to God the Father for everything, in the name of our Lord Jesus Christ." Ephesians 5:19-20

"I've yet to find the man, however exalted his station, who did not do better work and put forth greater effort under a spirit of approval than under the spirit of criticism." - Charles Schwab

"And this is my prayer: that your love may abound more and more in knowledge and depth of insight, so that you may be able to discern what is best and may be pure and blameless until the day of Christ, filled with the fruit of righteousness that comes through Jesus Christ--to the glory and praise of God. -Philippians 1:9-11

"If you want a quality, act as if you already had it." William James

"Each of you should look not only to your own interests, but also to the interests of others. Your attitude should be the same as that of Christ Jesus." Philippians 2:4

"The difference between a successful person and others is not a lack of strength, not a lack of knowledge, but rather a lack of determination." - Vince Lombardi

"I've got my eye on the goal, where God is beckoning us onward—to Jesus. I'm off and running, and I'm not turning back." Philippians 3:14 (The Message)

"Joy is the serious business of heaven" C.S. Lewis

"Rejoice in the Lord always. I will say it again: Rejoice!" Philippians 4:4

"The greatest weapon against stress is our ability to choose one thought over another." - William James

"Finally, brothers, whatever is true, whatever is noble, whatever is right, whatever is pure, whatever is lovely, whatever is admirable--if anything is excellent or praiseworthy--think about such things." Philippians 4:8

"Practice makes permanent." - Chris Beaty

"Whatever you have learned or received or heard from me, or seen in me--put it into practice. And the God of peace will be with you." Philippians 4:9

"Being challenged in life is inevitable, being defeated is optional." ~ Roger Crawford

"I can do everything through him who gives me strength." Philippians 4:13

"Kindness is the language which the deaf can hear and the blind can see." - Mark Twain

"Therefore, as God's chosen people, holy and dearly loved, clothe yourselves with compassion, kindness, humility, gentleness and patience." Colossians 3:12

"To forgive is to set a prisoner free and discover that the prisoner was you." Lewis Smedes

"Bear with each other and forgive whatever grievances you may have against one another. Forgive as the Lord forgave you." Colossians 3:13

"The most perfect technique is--one that is not noticed at all." Pablo Casals

"Let the message of Christ dwell among you richly, as you teach and admonish one another with all wisdom through psalms, hymns and songs from the Spirit, singing to God with gratitude in your hearts." Colossians 3:16-17

"The master in the art of living makes little distinction between his work and his play, his labor and his leisure, his mind and his body, his information and his recreation, his love and his religion. He hardly knows which is which. He simply pursues his vision of excellence at whatever he does, leaving others to decide whether he is working or playing. To him, he's always doing both." James Michener

"And whatever you do, in word or in deed, do everything in the name of the Lord Jesus, giving thanks to God the Father through him. Colossians 3:17 (CSB)

"Criticism has the power to do good when there is something that must be destroyed, dissolved, or reduced; but it is capable only of harm when there is something to be built." Carl Jung

"Therefore encourage one another and build each other up, just as in fact you are doing." 1 Thessalonians 5:11

"In our daily lives, we must make sure that it is not happiness that makes us grateful, but gratefulness that makes us happy."   - Albert Clarke

"Be joyful always; pray continually; give thanks in all circumstances, for this is God's will for you in Christ Jesus." 1 Thessalonians 5:16-18

"The time is always right to do what is right."
                    -Martin Luther King, Jr.

"...and as for you, never tire of doing what is right."
                    2 Thessalonians 3:13

"Do not think that love, in order to be genuine, has to be extraordinary." Mother Teresa

"The whole point of what I'm urging is simple: LOVE...love uncontaminated by self-interest and counterfeit faith, a life open to God." 1 Timothy 1:5

"There are no shortcuts to any place worth going." - Beverly Sills

"Do your best to present yourself to God as one approved, a workman who does not need to be ashamed…"   **2 Timothy 2:15**

"Of the thousands of pieces of advice, inspiration and encouragement I've received over the years, the most powerful one——the one that has played a central role in my life, both as a child and an adult——boils down to a single word: practice." Itzhak Perlman

Itzhak Perlman

"Study *and* be eager *and* do your utmost to present yourself to God approved (tested by trial), a workman who has no cause to be ashamed, correctly analyzing *and* accurately dividing [rightly handling and skillfully teaching] the Word of Truth." 2Timothy 2:15 Amplified Bible

"If all the world is stage...then perhaps we need a little more rehearsal." (Unknown)

"Be diligent in these matters; give yourself wholly to them, so that everyone may see your progress." 1 Timothy 4:15

"In the supermarket of life, everyone gets the cart with the bad wheel now and then." (Unknown)

"Watch your life and doctrine closely. Persevere in them, because if you do, you will save both yourself and your hearers." 1 Timothy 4:16

"God has no more precious gift to a church or an age than a man who lives as an embodiment of his will, and inspires those around him with the faith of what grace can do." Andrew Murray (South African pastor and writer, 19th century)

"Let us then approach the throne of grace with confidence, so that we may receive mercy and find grace to help us in our time of need." Hebrews 4:16

Tell me...and I'll probably forget. Show me...and I might remember. Involve me...and I'll understand. (Chinese proverb)

"In response to all He has done for us, let us outdo each other in being helpful and kind to each other and in doing good." (Hebrews 10:24)

"You're as close to God as you choose to be."

"Draw close to God, and God will draw close to you." James 4:8a (NLT)

"People say Sept. 11 changed the world. That is false. Thirty-three A.D. forever changed the world." Stanley Hauerwas (Duke University Theologian)

"Praise be to the God and Father of our Lord Jesus Christ! In his great mercy he has given us new birth into a living hope through the resurrection of Jesus Christ from the dead,"1 Peter 1:3

"Try not to become a person of success. Rather, try to become a person of value." – Albert Einstein

"...live in harmony with one another; be sympathetic, love as brothers, be compassionate and humble. Do not repay evil with evil or insult with insult, but with blessings, because to this you were called so that you may inherit a blessing. (1Peter 3:8-9)

"Adversity is like a strong wind. It tears away from us all but the things that cannot be torn, so that we see ourselves as we really are." Arthur Golden

And the God of all grace, who called you to his eternal glory in Christ, after you have suffered a little while, will himself restore you and make you strong, firm and steadfast. 1 Peter 5:10

"As long as you're green, you're growing. As soon as you're ripe, you start to rot." - Ray Kroc

"... grow in the grace and knowledge of our Lord and Savior Jesus Christ. To him be glory both now and forever! " 2 Peter 3:18

"Let no one ever come to you without leaving better and happier. Be the living expression of God's kindness: kindness in your face, kindness in your eyes, kindness in your smile."   - Mother Teresa

"Dear children, let us not love with words or tongue but with actions and in truth." 1 John 3:18

"Music is the only language in which you cannot say a mean or sarcastic thing." John Erskine

"Treat people as though they were what they ought to be and you will help them become what they are capable of being."   - Goethe

"Dear friends, let us love one another, for love comes from God. Everyone who loves has been born of God and knows God." 1 John 4:7

"I do not pray for success. I ask for faithfulness." - Mother Teresa

"..... Be faithful, even to the point of death, and I will give you the crown of life." Revelation 2:10b

Random Thoughts

The wind is like the air, only pushier.

When everything is coming your way, you're in the wrong lane.

Old Card Players never die, they just cut the deck.

An atheist is someone with no invisible means of support.

A rock store was closed by the police, they were taking too much for granite.

What is a computer's first sign of old age? Loss of memory.

"The Insomniac" by Eliza Wake

Notice! Take lettuce from top of stack, or heads will roll!

A letter carrier career is a mail dominated profession.

A guy goes into a second hand shop to buy one for his watch.

A job at the nursery can lead to a budding career.

The Italian government is considering installing a clock in the Leaning Tower of Pisa. The reason? What good is it if you have the inclination, but you don't have the time?

A farmer called his pig Ball Point. Well it wasn't it's real name, just a pen name.

When the unemployed actor got a job with a demolition company, he finally brought down the house.

Don't sweat the petty things and don't pet the sweaty things.

One tequila, two tequila, three tequila, floor.....

Atheism is a non-prophet organization.

I went to a bookstore and asked the saleswoman, "Where's the self-help section?"
She said if she told me, it would defeat the purpose.

What if there were no hypothetical questions?

If a deaf person swears, does his mother wash his hands with soap?

If someone with multiple personalities threatens to kill himself, is it considered a hostage situation?

Is there another word for synonym?

Where do forest rangers go to "get away from it all?"

What do you do when you see an endangered animal eating an endangered plant?

If a parsley farmer is sued, can they garnish his wages?

Would a fly without wings be called a walk?

Why do they lock gas station bathrooms? Are they afraid someone will clean them?

If a turtle doesn't have a shell, is he homeless or naked?

Can vegetarians eat animal crackers?

If the police arrest a mime, do they tell him he has the right to remain silent?

Why do they put braille on the drive-through bank machines?

How do they get deer to cross the road only at those yellow road signs?

What was the best thing before sliced bread?

One nice thing about egotists: they don't talk about other people.

Does the little mermaid wear an algebra?

How is it possible to have a civil war?

If one synchronized swimmer drowns, do the rest drown too?

If you ate both pasta and antipasto, would you still be hungry?

If you try to fail, and succeed, which have you done?

Whose cruel idea was it for the word "lisp" to have "s" in it?

Why is it called tourist season if we can't shoot at them?

Why is there an expiration date on sour cream?

Can an atheist get insurance against acts of God?

A day without sunshine is like night.

On the other hand, you have different fingers.

42.7 percent of all statistics are made up on the spot.

99 percent of lawyers give the rest a bad name.

Remember, half the people you know are below average.

He who laughs last, thinks slowest.

Depression is merely anger without enthusiasm.

The early bird may get the worm, but the second mouse gets the cheese in the trap.

Support bacteria. They're the only culture some people have.

A clear conscience is usually the sign of a bad memory.

Change is inevitable, except from vending machines.

If you think nobody cares, try missing a couple of payments.

How many of you believe in psycho-kinesis? Raise my hand.

OK, so what's the speed of dark?

When everything is coming your way, you're in the wrong lane.

Hard work pays off in the future. Laziness pays off now.

How much deeper would the ocean be without sponges?

Eagles may soar, but weasels don't get sucked into jet engines.

What happens if you get scared half to death, twice?

Why do psychics have to ask you your name?

Inside every older person is a younger person wondering, 'What the heck happened?'

Light travels faster than sound. That's why some people appear bright until you hear them speak.

Life isn't like a box of chocolates. It's more like a jar of jalapenos. What you do today, might burn your butt tomorrow.

Notice: Due to recent budget cuts and the rising cost of electricity, gas and oil, as well as current market conditions, the Light at the End of the Tunnel has been turned off.

Have you heard about the new alcoholic beverage that's on the market now? It's called Bourbon Renewal. After a few drinks your old neighborhood starts to look a lot better.

Riddles

What do you call cheese that isn't yours?
    Nacho Cheese.

What do you call Santa's helpers?
    Subordinate Clauses.

What do you call four bull fighters in quicksand?
    Quatro sinko.

What do you get from a pampered cow?
    Spoiled milk.

What has four legs, is big, green, fuzzy, and if it fell out of a tree would kill you?
    A pool table.

What lies at the bottom of the ocean and twitches?
    A nervous wreck.

Where do you find a dog with no legs?
    Right where you left him.

Why do gorillas have big nostrils?
>Because they have big fingers.

What do you get when you cross a pit bull with a collie?
>A dog that runs for help...after it bites your leg off.

What do you call a boomerang that doesn't work?
>A stick.

Why did the golfer buy a new club?
>Because he got a hole in one.

Why did the basketball player bring his suitcase to the playoff game?
>Because he travelled a lot

What did the doctor prescribe for laryngitis?
>The silent treatment

Why did the parents give their child a lot of educational toys?
>They wanted him to be a gifted child

Why do homemakers preserve extra fruit and vegetables?
>Because they can

What is the best way to communicate with a fish?
>Drop it a line

Why don't cannibals eat basketball players?
They dribble.

What do you call a nun who just passed her bar exam?
A Sister-In-Law

What do you have if you keep your canary in your automobile?
A flying car pet

Didja hear about the Broadway actor who broke through the floor boards?
He was just going through a stage.

WHAT IS IT?
It is greater than God.
It is more evil than the devil.
The poor have it.
The rich need it.
If you eat it, you will die.

ANSWER: Nothing.

ABOUT THE AUTHOR

Bobby Huguley is a Minister, Musician, Writer, Composer, Husband, Father, Grandfather, and sports fan. Having spent a career in local church music ministry, he has compiled an abundance of material to inform, inspire, and entertain musicians under his direction through the years. He lives with his wife Marsha in Myrtle Beach, SC.